HEROES REUNITED

A NOVEL BY

CHRISTINE E. SCHULZE

HEROES REUNITED

To Mrs. Daniels, my other Mrs. Fleming;
To Mrs. Fleming, my other Mom;
To Mom, just for being "Mom;"
To Sarah and Aaron, for being great best friends;
To all the rest of the Berean crew for being there too;
And, as ever, to Amiel for bestowing the blessing
Of such wonderful friends upon me

"Remember that Amiel is the Light of the world—He will be your Light when all other lights go out."

~Christine E. Schulze

"The Lord watch over me and thee, when we are absent one from another." (Genesis 31:49).

HEROES REUNITED

CHAPTER 1

Shadows swirled in his mind, and then they took form—black-cloaked men with onyx arrows, bows, and long, cruel, cold daggers...

Then, Chasmira running, stumbling through the darkness, fear-stricken eyes glancing constantly over her shoulder...

He reached out to her, the shadows descending, spiraling like terrible dreams out of control...

Drawing his sword, he swung at the Shadowmen as they surrounded Chasmira. They surrounded *him*. He kept attacking. To no avail. They swarmed, dragging him down, down, down. The madness of stifling shadows enshrouded him...

Aaron bolted upright in bed, panting, sweating, eyes luminous with terror. The nightmare had reoccurred—for the third, dreadful night in a row.

Springing from bed, he began shaking Nathan, Sam, and Josh.

"Guys, wake up," he urged, voice tremulous.

"Aww, man," moaned Josh, "it's, like, way too late for a midnight snack—"

"I'm sure he's not after food," Sam yawned. "Looks more like he's seen a ghost—"

"*Ghost? Where?*" Josh jumped to his feet. As everyone stared at him irritably, he added coolly, "Not that there's any such thing..."

"What's up, Aaron?" Nathan's brow furrowed as he studied his friend's pale, grave face.

"I had the dream again—about the shadows," he panted, struggling to control his breath, wishing it wasn't so blasted hot in their room as the sweat continued to cling to his body. He didn't tell them about Chasmira's part of the vision, not wanting them to grow as worried as himself. "It was so...real this time. Even more so than last time..."

"Oh, you mean when you woke me up from my ice cream dream—umph!"

Nathan elbowed Josh roughly before shaking his head at Aaron. "You *really* should talk to Mr. Root or someone about it."

"Or maybe a psychologist," Josh began, but stares from Sam and Nathan silenced him once more, especially as Nathan sighed very loudly, as if agitated that Josh didn't learn a thing from his violent elbow jab.

Aaron sighed, a great weariness suddenly pressing down on him. "It's probably nothing. I'll just have to trust Amiel and keep praying for answers, or at least some kind of peace. That's the best thing to do in any situation, right?"

"Right," agreed Nathan and Sam, yawning, though Josh's only reply erupted in a snore somehow louder and more obnoxious than his talking, as evidenced by both Sam and Nathan rolling their eyes.

As they all climbed back into bed, Aaron asked Amiel to show him His will concerning this new and yet seemingly haunting, old trouble, fervently hoping that His will didn't include the dream coming true.

CHAPTER 2

"Only three weeks left of school! Summer Vacation, woo! Only three weeks left of school!"

Josh carried about his usual business of shouting like a banshee and running madly on the school premises, catapulting through the dining common and spilling his fruit punch all over Krystal as he passed her.

"Josh White!" she shrieked, jumping from her seat and pursuing him. "You come back here so I can strangle your eyes out of your head!"

As everyone watched them with mild interest, Chasmira mumbled, "Remind me why he sits with us again?"

"Banned from Caleb's table," muttered Nathan.

"Yes, he out-pranked Caleb, something to do with eggs," Sam added.

"But he's sat with us for *months*. Shouldn't his banishment be over by now?"

"Guess he just likes sitting with us," Sam shrugged, "and he *is* our roommate. He has a right to."

Josh and Krystal presently returned and sat down calmly, Josh covered in jelly. Both looked unusually and nonchalantly satisfied.

"What—?" began Hailey, but Rachel held up her hand, declaring, "No, it's probably best not to ask."

"Aaron, you're awfully quiet," Chasmira voiced. "Something wrong?"

"No," he muttered.

"You've chopped up your pizza, been stirring it around for ten minutes, and your chocolate cake's still sitting there—uneaten—*unsampled*."

"I'm fine," Aaron returned stiffly.

"He hasn't been sleeping well." Nathan shoveled potatoes in his mouth. "Bad dreams."

"*Again?* What about?" Chasmira asked, concern flashing in her eyes.

"Nothing serious," he said casually, shrugging. If he hadn't even told the *guys* Chasmira was in his dream, he certainly wasn't about to tell *her* that he continued to envision black psycho-ninjas pursuing her.

"I'm sure it's nothing," he repeated.

"Oh, I understand." Hailey nodded solemnly. "I get those kinds of dreams. It's like when you dream about a roller coaster plunging into an endless chasm, and it does it over and over again, and you keep waking—"

"Zip it," snapped Rachel, and Hailey sighed.

Chasmira frowned. "Are you sure you're okay?"

"Yeah, sure." He tried to smile sincerely but quickly looked away as the worry did not dissipate from her eyes. Aaron wasn't known to lie. His honesty was one quality he knew she valued. Her eyes revealed her suspicion that he held something back, his secrecy bothering her more than anything...

A wad of potatoes smacked her on the cheek.

Rachel's eyes widened. She and the others stared at Chasmira whose lips pinched tightly together. Slowly turning her eyes upon a rather pale-looking Josh, she growled, *"What was that?"*

"Well, uhh, see, uhh, like, uhh, I was aiming for Krystal—"

"She's sitting right next to you—*on the other side*. How do you miss?"

"Uhh, I'm real sorry," he muttered sheepishly.

"It's alright." Chasmira coolly turned back to her food, though a mischievous grin tugged at the corners of her lips.

She suddenly retaliated with gravy, but as Nathan leaned forward to talk to Sam, it splattered across his face instead.

"Nate, I'm so sorry," she gasped dramatically, eyes wide, yet she could hardly refrain from laughing.

A long pause ensued in which everyone waited for the imminent to occur. And then, all at once, Nathan picked up an apple, Chasmira snatched a pickle to defend herself, and Hailey—who was, as ever, oblivious to what was about to occur—selected a pretzel and bit into it, smiling dreamily as Josh shouted, *"Food Fight!"*

A brief pause followed in which Mrs. Daniels, the solitary teacher in the room, rose to forbid this activity, but the next moment, the entire dining common broke into an uproar.

Krystal squirted jelly at every person she could. Nathan kept knocking Caleb in the head with apples—he was asleep, and Nathan found it very amusing to watch them bounce off his head, counting as he snored on unawares—and Sam was forced to dive under the table for cover since someone kept pelting him consistently with broccoli. Several people paused in their mashed-potato-and-jello-flinging to ogle at Rachel, who cried, "Aww, what a waste, people! I *love* broccoli!"

But then Rachel discovered the joys of grape-tossing, pelting them at Josh who continued to delight in flinging potatoes in people's hair, while Chasmira and Tiff both posed as gravy-slingers.

Aaron, however, was not in the mood to join in the madness, probably for the first time in his life. This was really a shame, considering such a good food fight hadn't occurred since the banana-pie-throw of last fall. Instead, he merely slipped off unnoticed—though not without getting squashed banana on his shirt, and he was actually quite fortunate this was the only wound he received—and headed for the boys' restroom.

He grabbed a paper towel, wet it, and began scrubbing the stain on his shirt. After several minutes, the stain was gone, and Aaron sighed, tossing the paper towel into the trash can. Was he *really* being too paranoid about this dream business? He was *never* too troubled to devour chocolate cake...

He studied his reflection in the mirror. Dark circles loomed beneath his eyes. He really hadn't been sleeping well at all. But then he noticed dark circles elsewhere. Gazing at the reflection of the door, he watched as shadows began forming all around its perimeter.

Swerving quickly, he tried to glimpse whatever it was, but at that moment, the door burst open, and the shadows vanished.

As a dozen or so boys all piled in, all thoroughly covered with various foods, Aaron shook his head, concluding the lack of sleep was causing him to hallucinate.

Turning to Caleb, he asked, "So, how'd it go?"

"Aww, man!" exclaimed Caleb, slapping his hand dramatically on the sink. "That was the greatest food fight in the school's history!"

Nathan sighed contentedly, "Yes, and it started at *our* table..."

"And our sister got bombed!" Josh rejoiced. "It was *so sweet!*"

"Someone attacked *Mrs. Daniels?*" Aaron blinked in disbelief. "Are they still alive?"

"Well, we're not sure who did it. She stood up to silence us—no one knows where Mr. Root was at the time—which didn't work, so she flew to the middle of the room to cast her angry laser glare at all of us, and right before everyone settled down, a piece of kiwi pie totally fell splat on her new blouse. She was hot —like, the mad hot, not the cute-hot, 'cause that would be disturbing if she was cute-hot, being my sister and all—not to mention a good kiwi pie was wasted, but then I guess watching her turn ten shades of livid was worth it..."

"Yeah," added Caleb, "and we're guessing Armond had something to do with it 'cause Mrs. Daniels failed him on his last English test..."

All the boys semi-cleaned-up by now, Caleb announced, "Well, best get back. That's the one bad thing about food fights—cleaning up afterwards without being allowed to use cleaning charms."

The boys filed out. Aaron remained at the sink, hands clutched to its basin. Taking in a deep breath, he determined not to allow the dream to bother him any-more and prepared to turn and leave when a low, hissing, cold whisper called, "Aaron..."

The lights dimmed eerily, the voice grew louder, more powerfully urgent, repeating his name faster and faster—

"Hey, Aaron, you coming or what?"

Nathan stood in the doorway, talking to him. Only Nathan.

"Yeah...sure..." Aaron gasped, realizing he was holding his breath. Releasing it, he walked rather briskly from the bathroom. As he paused to cast a final glance at the room, all appeared as it should be, no uncanny shadows in sight.

The dining common was quite a mess as Aaron entered it. The food wasn't restricted to floors, tables, and people's hair. A great deal of squashed fruits hung on the walls. Krystal painted her name in large, jelly letters on one wall, and someone else flew up to spray cheese wiz all over the ceiling.

Consequently, classes were forcibly pushed back, save Art which was can-celed altogether. Everyone felt relieved at this news, as Daniel exploded more pottery in the oven than not as of late.

Aaron, Armond, and Chasmira were last to leave. As they all cleaned separ-ate tables, Aaron stood lost deep in thought, mopping up punch and not even noticing two other people were there until Armond raced by, knocking a glass of lemonade on the table he wiped off.

"Sorry, Aaron!" he called over his shoulder, as the liquid poured all over. "Left something in my room and don't wanna be late for class!"

Aaron glared at the receding Armond before staring at the mess, sighing in frustration.

He jumped as someone's voice asked behind him,

"Need any help?"

He turned towards Chasmira.

"No, that's okay."

She swiped up a wad of napkins and began soaking the lemonade from the table.

"Thanks." He smiled a little.

As they continued cleaning, Chasmira continuously glanced over, as if noting his solemn, agitated expression. He knew she must suspect something. She was far from stupid.

Finally, she said, "Aaron, I'm worried about you. You're just not yourself. You haven't been all week."

Aaron sighed deeply and stared blankly at the table. He needed to tell someone how worried he was, so why not tell one of his closest friends, even if she thought him a complete lunatic?

"Chasmira, can I tell you something?" he asked in a low voice, as though fearing someone might overhear.

Chasmira studied his sharp, serious gaze carefully, replying quietly and with all sincerity, "Yes, Aaron. You know you can tell me anything."

"You won't tell anyone?"

She shook her head.

Leaning forward across the table, he lowered his voice to barely a whisper.

"You know those dreams I've been having?"

She too leaned in closer, eyes gleaming intently. "Yes."

"Well, it's not just that. I've been...seeing things...and hearing voices..."

11

Chasmira was silently pensive a few moments, trying to mask her discomfort. Yet he could feel the awkwardness as she bit her lip and furrowed her brow.

"Well...umm...have you talked to a teacher or someone about it?" she said finally.

"Do you think I should? I don't want to worry anyone..."

"I'm sure they'd understand. I mean, maybe you're just not getting enough sleep." She paused as he glinted skeptically at her. "But you believe it's all real, don't you?"

"I *know* it is. Whenever the voice speaks, shadows fill the room, like in my dream when—" He hesitated, for now did not seem like a great time to tell Chasmira he'd been dreaming of her getting swallowed up by random shadows. She was clearly shaken up already.

A horrified light crept into her eyes, and she gazed at him fearfully, breathing, "Aaron. What—what did the voice *sound* like?"

Before Aaron could reply, a cold laugh echoed throughout the room.

Chasmira's eyes, widely frantic, darted uneasily about. "What was that?"

They both looked up, feeling the darkness settle over them. Shadows merged and swirled on the ceiling like the warning rotation of an approaching tornado.

The voice declared in an ominous tone, "You have taken away my power, my glory, my authority—everything I held precious to me. Now watch as I take away everything that is precious to *you*..."

In an instant, the shadows vanished. Yet they stood staring in disbelieving horror at the ceiling, Aaron very pale, Chasmira shaking, a sick feeling grasping the pits of their stomachs. Suddenly, Mrs. Daniels entered, shooting them a sharp glance, making them jump while she announced that two minutes remained to get to class. She still looked quite irritable about not being able to remove the stain from her blouse. Chasmira and Aaron rushed to dispose of the paper towels, and then raced to History class. Yet before entering the classroom, they cast each other meaningful glances that revealed they shared a singular train of thought. They both heard the voice of Rorrim.

During History class, Labrier stepped outside to make copies of their assignments. Josh scowled at her as she departed, for she forgot their daily treat again, the licorice swirls she'd been promising for a week now.

Yet Aaron and Chasmira were oblivious to all else besides each other, what they just witnessed together. She scribbled a note and passed it to Aaron. Rachel saw and nudged Hailey, all the while gaping at Chasmira who was always too sickeningly obedient to pass notes.

After scanning the paper Aaron returned to her, she wrote back, *How can it be Rorrim? He was banished permanently.*

Aaron scribbled, *No idea. It's freaking me out, though.*

Chasmira scrawled, *I think we should tell Rachel and the others. We can trust them, and they'll want to know. They deserve it.*

Aaron seemed to mull over this last note a while before mouthing the words, *After classes, in the game room,* and Chasmira nodded.

After the final class was dismissed, Aaron, Chasmira, Rachel, Hailey, Nathan, Sam, Krystal, Tiffany, and Josh all made their way to the game room, Rachel all the while ranting between licks of her licorice swirl, which Labrier gave up after Josh finally blurted his injustice of never receiving his promised swirl. He received a mark for this outburst, but he only smiled proudly as he received both mark and swirl.

"Jikes!" Rachel cried. "What the heck is going on with you two, passing notes—?"

"Yeah, and not letting us see them!" Josh snorted.

"We'll tell you in the game room," hissed Chasmira, "just be quiet."

Yet as they entered the game room, they stopped short. It was packed with people.

"No privacy here," mumbled Chasmira.

"What about the garden?" suggested Aaron.

They all rushed to the garden, which was vacant save all the Thebaziles, Softshell turtles, and other creatures roaming about.

"*Now* will you tell us what's going on?" asked Rachel hotly.

Aaron and Chasmira quickly explained what happened in the dining common.

"No way!" Rachel exclaimed. "That Rorrim guy has more lives than a cat!"

"Huh?" asked Krystal. "What do you mean?"

"Well, we've already gotten rid of him, and now he's back hardly months later."

"We only did that once, and he was only *banished*," reminded Chasmira. "It's not like we killed him or something."

"Same difference," muttered Rachel, shrugging.

"You know, I never *did* understand that saying," mused Hailey, smiling as Rachel rolled her eyes.

"So, do you think we should tell Mr. Root or someone?" asked Sam.

"Well, we've got that field trip tomorrow," said Nathan slowly. "Why not wait 'til afterwards?"

Chasmira sighed. "What does a field trip have to do with anything?"

"Well..." Tiff rolled her eyes. "We were supposed to go dolphin skiing this one time and it was cancelled because of some false alarm about giants invading the school."

"Giants?" echoed Chasmira. "What crackpot made *that* one up?"

"Caleb," answered Josh, Krystal and Nathan in unison, and Josh chortled, "Heh, heh, my brother's a crackpot..."

"So," continued Tiff, "there's no need getting them all choked up, making them cancel the thing."

"Yeah," chimed Josh, "especially since I almost didn't even *make* the honor roll requirements for the field trip. Can you believe it?"

Everyone seemed to concur it was best not to answer this question.

"Tiffany's right," Chasmira agreed. "Maybe we should just concentrate on having a good time tomorrow at the Magic Mansion. Waiting a day won't hurt anything, right?"

Nathan suddenly started coughing as though he were about to choke, tossing his licorice swirl into a nearby bush.

"What's wrong?" asked Sam. "Did it try to bite you?"

"It tasted like vinegar and bananas."

"Hmm," mused Hailey. "Well, they *are* called '*surprise* swirls.' I had a pumpkin-ear-jam one once."

"Wish you'd warned me. I felt like—like—"

"Upchucking?" suggested Rachel, smiling slyly.

Everyone laughed, and momentarily forgetting their troubles, headed back to the game room for a wholesome, hazardous game of four-square.

CHAPTER 3

Every quarter, the students who made honor roll the preceding quarter were granted the privilege of going on a field trip, and today they headed off to the Magic Mansion. It was, as its name depicted, a huge mansion full of loads of fun activities, some of them strictly magically based, others scientifically based, like the huge electric ball you could place your hands on that made your hair stand on end while someone took your picture. Mrs. White always declared it was just as important to learn about regular science as it was to learn about magical science.

Some of the more magically based activities included the bubble room in which giant bubbles materialized out of thin air and you could step inside them and float about. The problem with this was that the bubbles were faulty and usually popped when you tried to get in. As the bus rolled along, Krystal bragged to Aaron that she stepped into one of the bubbles twice successfully, declaring she would do it again today. Aaron was all the while rolling his eyes and wishing very hard that he possessed a special ability of warping or invisibility. He tried to snag a seat with Chasmira, Hailey, Nathan, even Rachel, but he got stuck with Krystal for the forty-five minute drive because Josh set exploding turnips in the entrance hall. While half the people had already boarded the bus, the other half were doomed to temporary immobility and, apparently, second-rate seats once the madness cleared. Aaron marveled that Josh was even still allowed on the field trip. After all, who else, besides Caleb, also miraculously on the bus, would think to set exploding turnips in the entrance hall? Were the teachers that dense?

Aaron tried to ignore Krystal and think about what his favorite part of the field trip would be—the giant, winding slide that stretched from the top floor of the mansion all the way to the bottom—intermittently catching snatches of the other girls' conversations.

As they pulled up to the immense structure, Chasmira declared that this Magic Mansion was much huger than the Magic House she visited in Missouri. Rachel argued that "huger" didn't sound like a word, and Krystal was defending Chasmira by saying it *was* a word because she read it somewhere.

Aaron cut in, "Really? I didn't know you could read." Krystal stuck out her tongue, flipping her glossy hair superiorly over her shoulder, and Aaron rolled his eyes before uttering a prayer of thanks as the bus stopped. Mr. Root called for attention, thanked Amiel for safe travels, and all began piling out of the bus.

Aaron and the rest of the nine split off. The brightly colored entrance hall—which was like standing inside a giant aquarium, for the walls and ceiling were

16

made of glass, and fish swam all about them. Passing through, they came to the labyrinth room, which was actually several rooms combined to form a maze teeming with fun challenges such as using vines to swing over bottomless pits. The pits were an illusion, of course, but Josh did not realize this and prepared to turn back after gazing into one of the gaping holes, when he discovered that the prize for getting out of the maze before your other team members was a free scoop of ice cream. He then proceeded to move very quickly through the maze but got lost in the hall of mirrors and ended up back at the beginning. He was arguing with one of the Magic Mansion employees that he *had* gotten out of the maze before everyone else—that he came out the wrong end was clearly beside the point—and that they should post more clearly stated directions at the maze entrance, when Krystal showed up, declaring she would give him her ice cream if he would only shut up. After apologizing to the employee, she shoved the ice cream cone in Josh's hand and dragged him off.

Another favorite room was the weather room. It contained huge air vents which sent you soaring up into the air. The room also hosted clouds to stand under, and if you clapped your hands, the cloud would rain or snow on you. Rachel clapped a little too hard and found herself drenched heavily with rain. She walked away mumbling, "Jiminy cricket...for Pete's sake...so not coolio..." and every other annoyed expression she could surmise.

Everyone piled upstairs next, deciding they would come back downstairs later to play laser tag and try out the other games located on the main level. However, even getting upstairs proved a challenge. The staircase was very long and winding, and the stairs themselves disappeared the second after you stepped on them. So if you didn't run fast enough, a silverling fox Thebazile would catch you with its levitating powers and place you back at the foot of the stairs where you had to start all over again, as soon as the steps rematerialized.

Krystal soon grew quite agitated because Aaron, Chasmira, Rachel, Josh, Nathan, Sam, Hailey, and Tiffany all reached the top on their first try, after which she attempted the climb for a half hour.

"No, really, can't we just *leave* her?" Aaron whispered to Chasmira, but before she could answer, Krystal bounded to the top at last, holding her head triumphantly high.

The first room they found upstairs was the electricity room. Everyone had a chance to touch the giant electric ball, watch in a mirror as their hair stood on end, and get their pictures taken. Rachel's hair was by far the most amusing, with her bangs and ponytail sticking straight up. Antoine's turn came afterwards and proved a true disappointment. Everyone wondered why he tried it at all, as his little sister shaved his head and thus he possessed no hair to electrify. Josh voiced disappointment at not even seeing Antoine receive a good shock for his stupidity.

From the electricity room, Aaron's group moved to the kaleidoscope room. All four walls, as well as the floor and ceiling, were covered in colors and designs, and when you stood in the room and twirled, danced, or however you desired to move about, so did the colors and images. It was like being a part of the life-sized kaleidoscope itself.

Their next stop was the shadow room, in which a huge wall loomed. When you stood next to it, your shadow was displayed. You could strike a pose, a hidden camera would flash, and then you could stand back to admire the frozen shadow upon the wall. After a few moments, the shadows faded, and you could start over.

Chasmira and Rachel struck a pose that made a shadow which appeared as though they were kick-boxing with each other, and then Rachel and Aaron created several that depicted strangling each other. Krystal said that their strangling poses looked cool and very realistic, but then Aaron asked Krystal if he could strangle her too. Taking this a bit too literally, she suddenly announced she was off to find Tiffany for a game of laser tag.

Hailey was enjoying making shadow puppets with her hands when she was startled by Josh running and smashing into the wall, ricocheting off of it and falling backwards. As he stood up, rubbing his head where he pounded the ground, he explained he was trying to strike a jumping pose but "the wall got in his way."

The next room they explored was the bubble room. Everyone tried, with much annoyance and failure, to step into the huge bubbles as they materialized before them. But no one made any progress save Andrew the Washandzee who soon floated all the way to the vaulted ceiling. He couldn't figure out how to get back down, nor how to get out of the bubble which was surprisingly sturdy. But as he called for help, everyone just left the room, disgusted at his success in entering the bubble in the first place.

Next came the Morse code room which held a table with a partition in the middle. One person would sit on each side of the partition. Also, on each side sat a paper with a Morse code translation, a chalkboard and chalk, and a button that beeped when you pressed it. One person would beep a message, and the other would try to crack the code by looking at the translation of the letters and writing the words down on the chalkboard.

Aaron and Rachel were the first to have a go at it, but when Rachel figured out that Aaron was beeping random letters and numbers, she beeped in return, "You will pay," then proceeded to throw chalkboard erasers at him. Chalk dust flew and everyone cheered on until Mrs. Daniels entered the room and one of the erasers slapped her square in the face, knocking her glasses to the floor. They all stared in horror, but she only picked up the ruby spectacles and slipped them back on, shaking her head as she departed the room.

Nathan next challenged Aaron to a round of Morse code. After a half hour, they were still very involved in the beeping war they constructed over which was better—chocolate or caramel.

"Are you two gonna sit here arguing like loons all day?" Chasmira finally asked.

"Why not?" asked Aaron as he rapidly beeped, "At least chocolate doesn't get stuck in your teeth."

"What about the rest of you?"

No one answered her. They were too busy intently trying to decipher Nathan's next, wondrous, beeping retort.

"You guys promised we'd play laser tag, and half the day is gone already," she persisted.

"Erm...later," Aaron mumbled as he tried to figure out if Nathan just beeped "Caramel rules!" or "Caramel Drools!"

"Well, fine. If you're all gonna waste your day here, I'm gonna go find Anyta. At least *she'll* play laser tag with me..."

"Have fun..."

Chasmira headed for the giant slide, the only way to get downstairs, when footsteps sounded behind her. She stopped. So did the footsteps.

Finally, she turned.

"What do you want, Josh?" she growled at him.

"Umm...that's a very pretty blouse you're wearing."

She rolled her eyes and crossed her arms, sighing impatiently.

"I would be quite honored to escort you to the laser tag arena."

"Fine. Just stay away from me."

She started walking again, and he hurried his pace to catch up to her.

They found the slide, and as they sped down, Chasmira's shoe slipped off. She heard Josh crying behind her, "Ouch! Something hit me in the face," and forced back a laugh.

Once on the first floor, they found the laser tag arena where Kelsey, Anyta, Jarrett, Caleb, and a bunch of other people they didn't know were getting ready for a round of laser tag. Chasmira made certain to sidle over to Anyta's team as Josh joined the other.

They donned their laser vests, laser guns attached, then entered the immense room teeming with fake trees and fortresses. Someone announced over an intercom that they could begin as soon as the lights on their laser vests flashed. The moment their vests lit up, several people cheered—Josh rather loudly—as the game began.

"Let's split up," suggested Anyta, her teammates nodding in agreement before slipping into the dark shadows of the arena to await their prey.

It was Chasmira's first time playing laser tag, and she soon found it to be a thoroughly fun and rewarding experience. As she passed a Limonion boy on the opposite team, shooting his vest mercilessly as she went, Glory passed by, yelling at Armond that he tried to shoot her in the eye.

After several minutes of heartless attacking, Chasmira joined up with Anyta.

"The green team's meeting on the stairs," announced Anyta. "We should get a good shot at them from the windows up on the fortress wall."

"Okay."

Chasmira suddenly noticed someone passing before one of the windows and shot at the person. Flashing green lights told her she found her mark.

"Hey, you're not supposed to stalk people!" Josh ranted, thundering rather loudly around a corner before bolting up a ramp.

"What's he talking about?" sighed Chasmira. "I was shooting him, not stalking him—rules of the game."

Anyta rolled her eyes. "He's been saying that to everyone who shoots at him, vainly trying to accuse them of cheating, since he's such a bad player. He and Caleb made some kinda bet about who gets the least—"

Both girls felt their vests vibrate, and their green lights blinked guiltily.

They whirled to see a smiling Mrs. Daniels.

"Ha, ha!" she quipped, playfully triumphant as she scurried up a ramp, slipping from sight.

"We'll get back at her later," assured Anyta. "Let's go stalk Josh for real..."

* * *

While Chasmira enjoyed several games of laser tag, Aaron and Rachel delved into a heated argument in the Morse code room. Rachel was trying to convince him that "Spongy Triangle-Trousers" was a stupid, pointless cartoon that served only to melt kids' brains, while Aaron urged her that "My Little Ponyville" was created for the sole purpose of sapping little girl's brain cells and forcing female, cutsie stereotypes on them at young, far-too-impressionable ages.

Everyone else filtered from the room after about five minutes or so of this argument, dispersing to different rooms, Krystal muttering that the conversation itself was the most arguably stupid and pointless thing of all. Finally, Rachel gave up and chucked the chalk at Aaron's head. It widely missed, bouncing off of the window behind him. After adamantly declaring that she should've smashed the chalk board over his head instead, she stormed from the room in frustration.

After drawing a picture of Spongy Triangle-Trousers on his chalkboard, strictly for Rachel's benefit should she return to yell at him again as she often did, he stood and turned to walk away. But upon hearing a beeping noise, he paused and rolled his eyes. Did she come back so soon? Was she at it again already?

Yet as he turned and looked back, no one sat on either side of the partition. He glanced about cautiously, somewhat uneasily, before sitting back down.

Taking a piece of chalk, he carefully wrote out the message mysteriously sounded by the eerie beeps. "Hello, Aaron."

Fear gripped him, chills made his heart shiver. Some invisible person—if it even *was* a person—occupied this very room, speaking to him, separated from him by a sheer wall of fake wood, some stranger that knew his name. Aaron could feel a dark presence closing in slowly. This was definitely not one of Josh's or Caleb's pranks, though he wished for such a trick now more than ever.

Aaron spelled in return, "Who are you?"

The invisible hand replied, "You will find out soon enough. I would be more concerned about your friends right now, if I were you."

"My friends?" sounded Aaron.

"Yes," came the answer. "Where *are* the girls anyway?"

For a moment, he sat stunned by the horror of the noiseless words. Then he sprang up, rushing into the kaleidoscope room where Nathan was jumping, Sam waved his arms, and Josh performed some dance that looked like a cross between clumsy ballet and the hula.

"Nathan," he gasped. "The girls—they're in trouble—where's Chasmira?"

His troubled expression jerked them into reality. They rushed behind his heels as he returned to the Morse code room. Several people had entered, but none bore familiar faces.

"This is *not cool*."

Aaron stared at the place where the invisible hand spoke to him. He would've been grateful even to see Rachel right now. He tried to bring the dread slowly culminating inside him to a halt, tried to stave the sweat quickly spreading over his entire body. His mind needed to stay clear.

"Let's check the shadow room."

As Aaron, Nathan, Josh, and Sam raced into the shadow room, a flood of people flowed out of it, panic screaming within their eyes as they cried out frightfully, some stumbling over each other to get away.

As the boys stood watching, they saw no people, yet shadows remained, loads of dark shadows swirling upon the walls, seemingly *within* the walls. Even so, an iciness seemed to emanate from within those same walls. Suddenly, from the shadows leapt a dozen men. At least, they *looked* like men, but black clothes, including hoods and cloaks, concealed their identities. They drew long, slim, black swords which gleamed with dark intent, then slid past the boys, gliding rather than walking. As the boys watched, faces blanched with terror, Sam breathed, "What are they?"

"No idea," said Nathan shakily.

A scream shattered the air.

"Rachel," Aaron realized. "C'mon."

In the Morse code room, they found one of the Shadowmen fleeing with Rachel in his arms, his black cloak wrapped tightly around her.

Josh swiped up a piece of chalk and chucked it at his head, shouting, "Hey, ya moron, pick on someone your own size!"

The chalk merely bounced off his head harmlessly, yet he turned towards them. Several other dark-cloaked forms slithered forward, blades clutched tightly in hands concealed by black gloves gleaming with cold leather.

"Thanks a lot," mumbled Nathan. "Now they can kill *us* first—"

"Wait a sec." Aaron drew from his pocket a little, blue stone. "I summon Dianne, the fairy of Mira magic!"

In a bright, azure flash, Dianne appeared before them, griping, "This better be good. I was in the middle of the bestest book ever—whoa! You sure get into the biggest messes..."

"Just get us some weapons, will you?" snapped Aaron.

Dianne glowed brightly in concentration, and immediately they each wielded a crystal blade. They fended the Shadowmen off with their swords then started down the hall after the one who slipped from the room carrying Rachel. As they sprinted down the hall though, another scream echoed from a nearby room.

Jumping inside, they saw several Shadowmen descending from the shadows clustered about the ceiling, surrounding—

"Mrs. Daniels!" Aaron cried, but as the boys rushed to her aid, they stopped short to watch in awe, eyes wide, Josh's mouth gaping open.

Mrs. Daniels whipped a diamond ring from her pocket and placed it upon one of her delicate fingers. It glistened with brilliant rays of white light. As it glowed, her entire being glowed too, and then transformed. She stood draped in an elegant dress of rainbow silks, her hair longer, flowing freely in shimmering curls all about her, and two golden bracelets dangled upon each wrist.

"No way..." breathed Aaron. "I didn't *actually* think...Mrs. Daniels is Amanda Danielle?"

"Aww, man!" hissed Josh. *"You mean that hot fairy we met several months back is my sister?"*

"This is *not* the time, Josh," Nathan hushed him.

Amanda Danielle, whose violet-blue eyes teemed with concentrated determination, shot white balls of light at the Shadowmen, knocking a couple down and causing several to flee as they narrowly dodged the attacks. She called to the boys, "I've got things covered here. Find Chasmira and the others!"

Aaron led the way down the hall, wondering why he never noticed they were the same person, Mrs. Daniels and Amanda Danielle. They owned the same voice, looked nearly the same. Of course, perhaps it was the bizarre thought of someone sharing her youthful beauty being over a thousand years old, yet she *was* a fairy and a Scintillate.

Aaron paused, as did the others, as he caught a glimpse of Krystal in the room at the far end of the hall. Through the doorway, he could see her stepping into one of the bubbles carefully, impishly grinning, no doubt imagining her glee when she told Aaron she'd been able to step inside completely. Suddenly, the shadows clustered beneath her feet and swirled into the form of a dark portal.

Krystal shrieked as she saw the black hole, struggled desperately to get out of the bubble, to pop it, but she couldn't.

Aaron rushed down the hall towards her—Nathan, Sam, and Josh on his heels.

"Krystal!" Aaron called.

"Hurry!" she cried, eyes imploring him for one desperate moment before looking down horrifically upon the black spiral forming beneath her feet.

A shadow appeared in the wall, and from the wall emerged a Shadowman wielding a knife. He lifted it high— "No!" shrieked Josh—then brought it swiftly down, popping the bubble.

Down Krystal plummeted, her screams diminishing rapidly, even as she flew farther and farther from their grasp. As the Shadowmen jumped in after her, the portal snapped shut.

"Shoot!" Aaron shouted in frustration as they reached the spot.

"Aww, man..." Josh trembled as his face turned crimson. "When I find out who took her, I'm gonna—"

Another scream sliced the air, and all four boys glanced at each other knowingly. It was Rachel again.

"Look," said Aaron. "Let's split up Josh and I will try to find Tiffany and Chasmira, you two go after Hailey and Rachel."

"Sure," agreed Nathan, and they bolted different directions down the hall.

Sam and Nathan bounded towards Rachel's scream but suddenly noticed Hailey as they passed the electricity room and stopped to stare. One hand pressed firmly on the silver ball, her hair flying straight up on end, she somehow figured out how to take pictures of herself, strewing them all along the floor, ceiling, walls, everywhere. She seemed totally oblivious to the danger of the moment.

"Should we...?" began Sam.

"Let's leave her. She's out of danger for now, and she can always electrocute anyone who attacks her. Let's get to Rachel."

Rushing down the hall once more and rounding a corner, they spotted a half dozen Shadowmen, one with Rachel flung over his shoulders as she kicked, screamed, hit him in the back of the head, threatening to upchuck all over him if he didn't put her down.

The Shadowmen, silent yet swift, glided out of sight around another corner, and as Nathan and Sam rounded it also, the entrance to the slide gaped wide. Reasoning that the Shadowmen must've gone down, they prepared to follow when Hailey raced by, hair still standing on end, and dived down the slide herself. A Shadowman pursued, and the boys leapt down the slide after them.

The slide proved exceptionally long, windy, and very fast. Nathan cried out at some point that he lost a shoe, to which Sam replied, "Yeah, thanks, it just thwacked me in the nose."

Eventually, the slide straightened. Their eyes widened as they saw Hailey plummeting straight towards a Shadowman as he climbed up the slide, a very awkward-looking antic for an evil, cloaked entity to be performing. The boys couldn't draw their swords, and if they did, they were more likely to spear Hailey than the Shadowman. Yet as Hailey came to the end of the slide, she stuck out her hands and touched the Shadowman who vibrated and toppled over, stunned.

"Wow, you were right," began Sam, but he stopped short as another black portal opened at the end of the slide. Sam dove over Nathan, grabbing desperately at Hailey. He only managed to fall and bang his chin roughly, kicking Nathan in the lip who yelled loudly while Hailey slid right into the portal. It snapped shut behind her, vanishing.

Meanwhile, Aaron led Josh back to the first floor.

"Where are we going?" asked Josh.

"Laser tag room—I remember Chasmira saying she was gonna go there for a while."

As they tried to enter the laser tag room though, a lady shouted, "Hey, you can't go in there without paying!"

Aaron turned, handed the scowling woman some money, muttered, "Have a great day," and bolted into the laser tag room.

As they donned laser vests and guns, Josh stared at Aaron. "Dude, you just totally gave her a twenty dollar bill."

"No time to worry about that." Aaron secretly reminded himself to kick himself in the head later though. How many ice cream cones he could've bought Chasmira—if he ever saw her again. *No.* He shook his head, refusing to think that way...

They entered the laser tag room where everyone was still shooting at full throttle.

"Dianne?" called Aaron.

"Hmm? What?" she mumbled from the top of his head where she slept, miraculously without falling off.

"Could you please activate these?"

"Hmm? Sure." She lazily pointed at the laser guns and vest, and the lights on them glowed to signify their turning on.

"What about the—?" began Aaron.

"Yes," mumbled Dianne, "I have efficiently equipped them so that if you shoot at the Shadowmen, they will injure them, but otherwise they are normal laser guns and will not...harm...other...people..." She drifted back into dreamland as Aaron felt her roll over on his head, grabbing at a tuft to use as a makeshift blanket.

"Man, this place is *huge*," said Josh as they started up a ramp, staring at the massive fake trees and boulders. "Should we split up—?"

A scream pierced the air.

"C'mon!" shouted Aaron as they rushed towards the source of the shriek. Rounding a corner, they found a Shadowman grabbing Anyta by the arm. She stared at him dumbfounded, expression eerily vacant, apparently unable to move or speak. As Aaron and Josh rushed towards her though, the Shadowman took off.

"Boy, we must look pretty intimidating," Josh smirked.

"No, it's not that. I think they were looking for something..."

"Are you okay?" Josh asked Anyta.

"Yeah..." Her gaze lingered distantly a few moments more, then the haziness melted back into reality, and she shook her head. "He was looking into my eyes —it was like being in a trance or something..."

"Did you see which way he went?"

"Well, he sort of disappeared through that cardboard tree over there."

"Thanks. You sure you're okay?"

"Yeah, I'll be fine."

As Josh and Aaron bounded back down the ramp, Aaron muttered, "See, they don't want to capture *all* the girls..."

As he said it, Rorrim's words echoed in his memory, "Now watch as I take away everything that is precious *to you...*"

A petrified cry pierced Aaron's heart, draining his skin to the palest white.

Chasmira. Aaron's dream flashed in his memory, threatening to let the fear consume him once more, but he knew he couldn't let that fear take hold. He ran faster after her cries. As he and Josh raced down the ramp, Nathan and Sam joined them, Nathan explaining, "Hailey's captured, and we saw one of the Shadowmen carry Rachel in here."

"And they've got Tiffany too," added Sam. "She disappeared with one of the Shadowmen into the kaleidoscope room."

They came in sight of a dozen or so Shadowmen, two carrying hostages—Rachel, who really did look as though she might upchuck any moment, and Chasmira, her face the palest shade of white, eyes wide as saucers.

"Hey, you cowards!" Aaron screamed after them. "Come pick on someone your own size!"

"Oh, you mean us?" said Nathan. "Cause we're kinda shorter, and we might not wanna encourage them—"

He was cut off as several Shadowmen bore down upon them. Swords clashed, metal sang, and the boys shot white jets of light from their laser guns. Dianne woke up, kicking the Shadowmen in the head, which didn't really hurt them but distracted them somewhat, seeming to grant her great pleasure as she shouted passionately, "Take that, you great bullies!"

After only a few minutes, the Shadowmen lay stunned or injured at their feet —but where were the girls?

Aaron wasn't the only one who felt it now—a cold, ominous, hopeless dread rushing over them. They looked up. The last two Shadowmen sped rapidly towards a dark portal that just opened at the end of the hallway. The boys tried to move but found they suddenly couldn't, forced to stand frozen, staring in horror as their two friends disappeared into the shadows. The last thing Aaron saw was Chasmira gazing at him with a fear-ridden face that called to him, yet there was nothing he could do but stand and watch her painfully slip away from him.

Finally, all lay silent, the shadows vanished. But it was not a peaceful silence, for the room was no longer filled with the girls' smiles, their laughter, their idle chatter now a seemingly precious treasure lost. Aaron did not know how or where, yet he determined he must not let Rorrim, however he was involved, to get away with his horrid crime. He would not let his last memory of Chasmira become that look of pleading horror because he could not save her.

CHAPTER 4

As he turned to face the other boys, the same look of determination, of a new courage they never felt before, flared upon their faces as well. But then they all glanced at each other with the same, questioning look. Where would they begin?

They did not have to wait long for an answer, for someone commanded behind them, "Boys, come with me."

Turning, they saw Amanda Danielle standing very tall, looking upon them with intense seriousness.

"The time has come."

She pointed the finger on which the diamond ring perched at the floor. A ring of light appeared underneath each of their feet, and then the light enveloped them. Suddenly, they left the Magic Mansion, and darkness surrounded them. As Amanda Danielle shouted, "Illuminate!" a bright light emanated from her ring until it filled the whole room with light. They stood in a huge cave. The boys recognized it at once as the Fairy council of the Spectrum Isles.

"I see you remember the place," Amanda Danielle began. "This place has become a home for many magical artifacts. It is here I found the stones."

"Stones?" Nathan echoed.

"Yes. Aaron, pull out your summoning stone."

Aaron pulled the blue stone from his pocket.

"These stones are what Rorrim seeks. I gave each of the girls one to protect at the end of your last quest. I too carry one with me."

As she held out her hand, the diamond ring glistened.

"Whoever holds one or more of these stones in his or her hands has the power to summon a great army. If Rorrim obtains them, he will summon a great Army of Darkness. Already, he holds one of them and is using its strength to summon every bit of evil power and dark alliances to himself that he can, such as the Shadowmen. Since he is banished and cannot leave his castle to cause evil, he will bring all the evil he can to himself.

"Do not worry for the girls though. So long as they keep their stones with them, Rorrim cannot harm them. He knows this. He will *try* to get the stones from them, but he cannot *force* the stones from them. He would have to trick them into it, for summoning stones must be given up willingly by their guardians, and I do not believe the girls would be so foolish as to give the stones to him.

"Now, you must go to the Island of Utter Darkness, where Rorrim's castle is situated. When you reach the castle, use the stone to summon one of the Armies of Light, attack Rorrim, and save the girls. In the meantime, I will try to get the other stones to you. I would give you mine now, but the right time is not yet come. I may need it to help the girls before my quest's end.

"My ship rests on the eastern banks of this island. It is a magic ship, you need only steer the wheel and worry about nothing else. It will stop of its own accord to avoid crashing into the shore. You must sail due east to reach the Island of Utter Darkness. You may start in the morning. I want you each to get a full night's rest, for you will need it for tomorrow's trials.

"One last thing. Rorrim will send dark enemies and obstacles in an attempt to thwart your mission, once he knows you're on the way. Your common shields and swords will not suffice though." Swords appeared in sheaths about their waists, shields strapped upon their backs. "You must equip yourselves with the same great weapons the Armies of Light wield.

"And so I have found and brought with me..."

With a snap of her fingers, seven arrows hovered in their midst, sparkling like precious stones, each a different color—purple, indigo, blue, green, yellow, orange, and red.

"Ancient gifts of the Colorz sisters. They've been reserved here for some time. The seven sages of Spectrum thought it appropriate to keep them in honor of the Heroes of Light, for when they should each have need of them..."

The boys suddenly noticed the bows they held in their hands. They received the gifts with silent reverence, gazing at them in awe yet with a heavy solemnity, realizing the battle stretching before them, a battle they must face if they wished to save the girls.

"Now, Aaron, you take the violet, Nathan the red, Josh the yellow, Sam the green, and I'll take the rest."

They each grabbed their assigned arrows, setting them to their strings while Amanda Danielle poised the remaining three on her bow.

"Now, on the count of three, aim the arrows at each other and shoot them into the air. Ready? One—"

They stretched back their bow strings.

"Two—"

They slowly pointed the arrows upward, aiming the points so they would meet in the air when released.

"Three!"

The arrows sped, crashing into each other and exploding in a flash of sparkling, white light, like a dancing firework.

White, glittering dust fell all about them, causing their shields and swords to glow and turn pure gold, while in their midst hovered seven, white arrows. Their bows shone with a brilliant white as well.

"Each of you take one arrow to use," continued Amanda Danielle. "They will regenerate as soon as you use one.

"One, last thing before we go. Remember to use the medallions I gave you should you have need to prove your loyalty to me or the Armies of Light. I doubt you shall meet anyone but foes on your quest, but keep the medallions close nonetheless. You never know when an unseen friend may lurk near, protecting you.

"Now, we must get back."

In a flash, they left the cave and stood in the boys' dormitory.

"I have much thinking and praying to do now," Amanda Danielle declared. "I leave you now to do the same as well. I shall be in my room if you should need anything."

CHAPTER 5

Aaron found Amanda Danielle sitting on her balcony, gazing up into the stars. Her eyes traveled far, deep, pensive. He wondered if he should disturb her, but many thoughts pressed on his mind. At any rate, he was certainly incapable of heeding her command to get a good night's rest.

She looked up. "Is there something I can do for you, Aaron?"

Walking over, he sat beside her.

"Mrs. Daniels." He caught the stare of those strong, clear, blue eyes for a moment, and then looked down again. "It's just, well, traveling into a world of utter darkness...Well, I guess Lynn Lectim was covered in darkness once so it's not really *that* which bothers me, it's just...the last time we just had to *banish* Rorrim. This time we actually have to destroy him...*kill* him in a battle..."

He couldn't quite bring himself to admit he was scared in front of Amanda Danielle though he knew she *did* understand, as evidenced in her careful reply, "It is wise to fear some things and know the danger of certain things. I admit that I am frightened as well, but..." She gently took his hand, and he looked up at her soft yet powerful gaze, her eyes full of intense urgency. "... we must not let those fears overcome us."

Aaron looked away again. He knew he worried too much instead of praying and placing the matter in Amiel's hands. Sometimes though, that seemingly simple task was so truly difficult to carry out.

"Aaron," Amanda Danielle continued softly. "When Rorrim said you took away what was precious to him, he meant power, riches, glory, authority— worthless things of the world that shall fade away. But *you*—you treasure those things which really do matter. First of all, you love Amiel. Secondly, you value friendship, truth, forgiveness, love—you are already very wise for one your age.

"Only remember that Amiel is not only your Savior, but the King of your life. He has saved you from all wrongs, from an eternal death, and He can save you from your daily troubles and help you through your daily trials as well. If you are afraid, you can give all your troubles to Him, and He will be there to guide and comfort you. Remember that Amiel is the Light of the world—He will be your Light when all other lights go out.

"And you must have courage. Courage is not being fearless. It is being willing to face and overcome your fears because some things are more important than being afraid, such as saving your friends. Saving Chasmira."

Aaron remained silent. He was still digesting all of Amanda Danielle's counsel. She was right. Amiel protected himself as well as all the others this far. All he needed was to trust Amiel to continue protecting and leading them. And even if he died in the process of saving his friends, it didn't matter, as long as Rorrim was defeated and his friends rescued. As he thought these things, a feeling crept into his heart, a feeling he was sure came from Amiel alone, a secret knowing they would succeed.

Finally looking up at Amanda Danielle, he smiled.

"Would you like me to pray with you?" she asked.

"Yes," he decided quietly, "I'd like that."

* * *

"Sis?"

Amanda Danielle heard a voice behind her, and turning her head, saw Josh enter. She smiled at him sadly.

Josh sat beside her, asking quietly, "You okay?"

"Sure." She again gazed out into the stars. "Just...thinking..."

Josh studied her silently. She stared into the stars as if reaching deep, deep into the recesses of her mind, as if each star was some sacredly buried memory.

"Josh, my name isn't 'Daniels.'"

"What?" He stared at her perplexedly.

"My last name—haven't you ever wondered why it's 'Daniels,' and not 'White,' like the rest of the family?"

"No, Mama always said it was 'cause she was married to someone else before she married Dad, and when he died, you kept his last name."

Amanda Danielle smiled at him sorrowfully. "It's true that my real father *did* die, but that is not the reason for my name...

"Josh, I have been thinking. It has been wrong for us—for *me*—to keep these things secret from you and Caleb and the others all these years...

"Josh, I once had a fiancée."

33

Josh stared. A thousand questions popped in his mind. "A *what?* But how, when?"

"It was long ago, over 1,000 years, yet I remember it as though it was yesterday...

"Papa—that is, Eliot, my birth father—and Mama were the high king and queen of Iridescence. It was during the time of Loz—before Zephyr's Islands were formed. I was the eldest of three. I had a brother, Elisha, and a sister, Gwendolyn—"

"No way!" Josh cried. "Are you saying *the legendary Elisha and Gwendolyn—that we're, like, half-siblings of them?*"

Amanda Danielle smiled slightly at his enthusiasm.

"The very same."

As Josh gawked and gaped in disbelief, Amanda Danielle continued, "At that time, Papa was very ill. He was dying. Even the great healers could do nothing for him. Mama was planning to go to the Vale of the Mira after his death. Her cousin was the queen there and never married, nor thus left any heir to the throne. She left everything, including the throne, to Char, my mother—our mother. And so Mama would have to move there and become queen, and as the eldest, I must take over the throne of Iridescence. But it was law in those days—before Chryselda was queen and changed such laws—that the princess must marry before she could be crowned queen and gain the inheritance.

"And so I met *him*, the prince of the Prismatic people. But at the same time, the Destiny Stone, the emerald which I ultimately gave to Aaron, came into my possession, and a great enemy sought to take it from me..."

Her voice trailed as the scene flashed in her memory...

"Go now to safety, Mandy, and I will come for you someday—I promise. Someday you shall stand in your tower and gaze out the window towards the east, and from there you shall see me coming."

"Then I shall wait," she said softly, the tears choking back her words. She clasped the ring strung about her neck. *"I shall wait..."*

"'I will wait,' I said, and then I jumped out the window onto the phoenix. As we flew, I turned back...and my prince fell out the window...into the fire below...that was the last, awful glimpse I saw of him..."

Josh handed his sister a tissue as the tears sparkled in her eyes and trickled down her cheeks. He never before saw his sister in such sorrow, and he tenderly put his arm around her. At first, he felt a bit awkward extending this small comfort—he didn't usually go around hugging his sister, if he could help it—but as she offered him a slight smile, he smiled back, listening intently as she continued,

"After that, I went to the Vale of the Mira and told Mama everything. The Garden of Endless Light was built nearby in the woods, its purpose to protect me —and the stone—'til the hero came to claim it. I received many daily visitors, but I was sick with a different kind of loneliness. Each day, I sat in my tower, hoping to see him come riding upon a valiant white steed, but...he never came...

"I finally concluded that he was dead, though in my heart I knew I would never love another as I loved him. So I took his name for my own, and now I am Amanda Danielle Daniels.

"As I prayed, Amiel revealed my need to focus on my purpose for coming to the garden. I must protect the stone until the Hero came to obtain it. After Aaron came, I again sought Amiel's will for my life, and He led me to the Spectrum Isles where I became one of their sages—and again became involved in fighting against Rorrim who was stirring trouble there at the same time as he stirred up trouble at Lynn Lectim in the future. I remained in Spectrum a long time. Then, finally, Amiel led me down a different path—and eventually it would lead again to Aaron and the fight against Rorrim. I graduated from the Lynn Lectim School and have taught there ever since."

So many questions bounced in Josh's head that he wasn't sure which to ask first. He especially didn't wish to breach too tender a subject, seeing the great waves of pain already swelling in his sister's eyes as she remembered.

"Wow...well, umm, what about Mama? When did she leave the Mira and become a teacher?"

"Well, while she was queen in the Mira Vale, she met and married Douglas, our father. They had one son before you and Caleb. His name was Zach. When he was twenty-five, they set him upon the Mira throne and entered into the Kalvyrie ministry full-time after praying and believing it to be Amiel's will for their life. Zach married and had a daughter—Liv. But then Zach and his wife both died in a terrible murder. Some thought Rorrim was involved with it...

"Anyhow, I often sent letters to Mama and Papa, and they returned them frequently. Yet when my letter did not come for a while, they grew worried. They did not know I was being held a prisoner of Rorrim, during the time I posed as one of the sages of the Spectrum Isles. I did not tell them in my last letter where I was going. It was very foolish of me. All those years they looked for me, searched for me, worried over me. After I was rescued, I searched for them as well. We did not find each other until one hundred years after my release. They looked for *two hundred years*. The reunion...you can't imagine how happy we were...

"When we returned to Iridescence, Chryselda and Elisha were on the throne. We stayed with them a little while, but after seeing the kingdom was in good hands, moved to a cottage in Forest-foot and have lived there ever since. It was then I became a teacher, and so did Mama, while Father became a spiritual leader amongst Amielians—a Pastyre."

Josh had been listening intently. Now he scratched his head, still thinking. A myriad of questions yet swirled in his mind, but he wondered if he should ask them. Slowly, he ventured, "Sis, could I ask...how did you and the prince meet? I mean, if you don't want to—"

"No, it's alright." She sighed deeply, and the sad smile flowed like a deep wave drowning her eyes. "It all began when—"

A sudden noise like the flapping of great wings boomed. Amanda Danielle and Josh both scanned the sky, Josh's fingers inching towards the hilt of his sword.

Silence enshrouded them, and yet, it seemed darker, it *felt* darker. As if they were not alone.

Suddenly, Josh brandished his sword, exclaiming, "Sis, look out behind you!" before a black cloak flung over his head, blinding him.

CHAPTER 6

"I say we pack up some food and leave tonight," declared Nathan.

"You heard Mrs. Daniels—err, Amanda Danielle—err, whatever." Sam shook his head. "She wants us to get a good night's sleep and start out re-freshed."

"Let's face the facts," said Aaron. "None of us is going to get a decent night's sleep until the girls are back here with us."

Josh burst in, his face paler than the death-cold moon looming in the win-dow behind him, stark white in terror.

"Josh." Sam frowned concernedly as they all stared at him. "What's wrong?"

"They've taken her," Josh uttered, trembling.

"Who?" demanded Aaron sharply.

"He took my sister—he took Amanda Danielle—"

"*What?*" blurted Nathan. "Who? When? Where—?"

"Just now, on the balcony. There must've been two of 'em, 'cause one, like, blinded me with his cape. I fought him off, but when I looked up, she was gone, and so were the Shadowmen."

The boys all glanced fearfully at each other and then at Aaron. He lowered his head as if entering deep thought and prayer. They needed an answer about what to do. They needed one fast.

"The ship!" he exclaimed. "If the Shadowmen took the girls to the Island of Utter Darkness, they probably took Amanda Danielle there too. Sam, run to the kitchen and fill your backpack with as many sandwiches or whatever food you can find. Nathan, you take our water containers and fill 'em. Josh—"

Aaron noticed how shaken up Josh still appeared, shaking frantically and blanching so pale he might pass out any moment. "I'll stay with Josh. We'll make sure everyone's bows, quivers, and arrows, are ready. You all still got your swords and shields on you?"

They all nodded.

"Good. We'll meet back here then head down to the ship. But hurry!"

As Nathan and Sam scuttled from the room, Aaron turned back towards Josh as he collapsed on the edge of the bed, trembling violently all over. He held his face in cupped hands, tears streaming beneath his fingers.

"Hey, Josh." Aaron sat beside him, awkwardly placing a comforting hand on his shoulder. "Hey, man, it'll be okay..."

"I'm sorry," Josh sputtered. "I–It's just...the kind of thing you think will never happen, you know?"

"I know," Aaron breathed, then added more determinedly, "We'll find them, alright? We'll find them..."

* * *

The four boys paused to observe the dismal sight. The morning sky stretched cold and gray, like a dead man's shroud as they reached the ocean shore. The ship itself, which looked as though it was made of pearl, covered from head to foot with white, glistening lilies, radiating a pale, white sheen. It rested in the waters gleaming like smooth, black glass, dark and unfriendly. The sky was strewn with gray clouds. The only light shone from the blooming lilies masking the ship.

"Come on," Aaron commanded quietly, the others following solemnly.

They boarded the ship and began the trip across the dark waters, taking turns at the wheel. No wind blew, not even the slightest breeze, and their progress was slow.

As the day drew on, the clouds grew darker. Then, in the distance, they could make out the dim form of some flat surface—The Island of Utter Darkness. Over it hung black, impenetrable clouds. A great shadow clung to the land and the still waters surrounding it. As they approached the shadow, the air grew hotter and denser. The place smelled thick with evil. Aaron wrinkled his nose. He would've never considered evil owning its own smell, but Rorrim's presence was drenched with it—so was the atmosphere entrapping this place.

They passed the borderline into the shadow, at first reeling dizzily. The initial shock of the great evil surrounding them was a powerful one. However, upon regaining full capacity of their senses, they noticed that all the lilies on the ship folded their petals, their dim light completely fading. Their light did not shine powerfully enough to fight the evil they faced now. As the island neared, they knew for certain they just made the most pivotal decision of their life. There was no going back now.

CHAPTER 7

Chasmira, Rachel, Hailey, Tiffany, and Krystal all gazed about the small, uppermost room of the tower. Their emotions mixed fear and curiosity as they gazed about the poorly furnished room. The room contained only three mattresses, a bed, a small table, and a large, old wardrobe, the finish of which looked very old and distressed.

When their nerves somewhat settled, the five girls took their seats on one of the mattresses, setting their purses and back-packs on the other.

"Okay," Chasmira finally broke the silence. She took a deep breath. "Let's evaluate what we know so far."

"Well, we're in some huge, dark, castle thing-a-ma-bob of Rorrim's." Hailey's eyes surveyed the room with bright amusement.

"And he questioned each of us separately, demanding we give him 'our powers,'" Krystal added.

"Which is insane since we don't have any," Rachel grumbled irritably. "Not to mention he must be attempting to starve us, considering we've been here for hours with no food."

She pulled out a cross-stitch project from her backpack and jabbed the needle through the cloth, as if inwardly pretending it was Rorrim's face.

Hailey began rummaging through her backpack and suddenly exclaimed, "Oh! I forgot I packed loads of food. You know, in case the bus broke down, or —"

She stopped as Rachel's head shot up, her eyes flaring wildly at Hailey.

"You mean you had food all this time and you didn't *tell* me—err, us?"

"No, guess it slipped my mind," Hailey chuckled.

"Why, I oughta—" Rachel lunged at Hailey, but the other three girls held her back, as if fearful she really might throttle Hailey.

Rachel took to kicking holes in the poorly constructed walls instead, imagining them to be Rorrim's shins, while Tiff kept repairing them.

Rachel's scuffle with the wall was interrupted, however, as the door opened and two soldiers forced a struggling person into the room before shutting the door behind them once more. The protesting captive fell onto one of the mattresses in her struggle to break free. The girls gasped as she looked up.

"Amanda Danielle?" Chasmira finally managed to breathe. "How did you —"

She held up a diamond ring which glowed, and suddenly Mrs. Daniels stood before them.

The girls all gawked, completely speechless.

"Yes, Mrs. Daniels and Amanda Danielle are one." The young fairy returned to her Amanda Danielle form. "And someday I will get to tell you how I came to be Mrs. Daniels and tell you all my secrets. However, now is not the time. There are more important matters at hand.

"As you know, we are all captured in Rorrim's fortress, but I reassure you that Rorrim will do us no harm. Also, Aaron, Nathan, Sam, and Josh are on their way even now to rescue us."

"They won't make it," sulked Rachel. "When Rorrim was interrogating me, he said that we're in the middle of a desert, and it's too hot to cross unless you know the secret ways."

"He told me there was this dreadful ocean to pass over to get to the island." Krystal closed her eyes, shuddering. "Poor Josh in that cold, dark place."

"But the boys can do it," Chasmira said confidently, though her eyes betrayed her fear. "They—they've been on quests before. Well, Aaron has, at least."

"But not such serious ones," Tiff pointed out.

"We must not despair," reminded Amanda Danielle. "Rorrim tells you these things because he knows your weaknesses and wants to break your spirits, destroy your courage. But you must not let him."

As if noting the doubtful, frightened looks on each of their faces, she decided not to discuss their situation further.

"It is late. Let us all pray together and get some sleep. We will talk more in the morning."

* * *

"It'll be alright, Rachel." Chasmira laid Rachel's head in her lap, stroking her red hair. Rachel lay whimpering in her sleep for some time now, her mind heavily plagued by nightmarish visions.

After an hour, all the girls finally lay fast and peacefully asleep. All but Chasmira, to whom sleep would not come. She made her way to the window and sat staring into the black, starless sky, doing what she longed to do more than anything. She cried. She saved her tears 'til they all slept soundly, not wishing to break any of their spirits. She was the eldest, even if only by a few months—thus she felt a stark obligation to be brave and strong. But in reality, she was scared just as the rest of them.

A gentle hand touched her shoulder and a gentle voice whispered her name. Looking up, she saw Amanda Danielle's gentle face smiling sadly down at her.

Sitting beside Chasmira, she asked, "What's troubling you, Chasmira?"

"Mrs. Daniels, I—I'm afraid. I'm afraid for the boys—afraid for Aaron— what if they don't make it? We don't know where they are—?"

"I'm sure the boys are fine. I'm sure they're headed to the island on my ship even as we speak. We must pray for them and trust Amiel to keep them safe. 'The Lord watch over me and thee, when we are absent one from another.' Everything will work out for good."

Chasmira smiled, and Amanda Danielle embraced her before prompting, "Now, do you think you can sleep?"

"Yes, Mrs. Daniels...thank you."

Amanda Danielle grinned in reply as Chasmira crawled into the bed besides Rachel. Amanda Danielle breathed her own prayer for the boys before retiring to bed, knowing they would need Amiel's help. Many dark trials awaited them.

CHAPTER 8

Morning dawned. Everyone awoke refreshed and in better spirits, especially after Hailey provided them each with fruit for breakfast from her teeming backpack. Afterwards, Amanda Danielle announced it was time to "get down to business" and tell them further of their situation.

"Rorrim seeks nine stones called the 'Summoning Stones.' If combined, these stones could summon an army great enough to overthrow Zephyr's Islands in one, foul swoop. This is the plan that has been forming in Rorrim's wicked heart for some time now.

"However, if the stones land in righteous hands, the army summoned shall be righteous, the great Army of Light which could overthrow Rorrim and his forces.

"Rorrim has been using the one stone he possesses to draw as many evil servants and power to him as he can.

"Aaron too owns one of the stones, the blue topaz given to him by Dianne. One...I do not know what has become of it...but we must get the six, other stones that we possess to Aaron as quickly as possible."

"*We?*" echoed Rachel, but something cold suddenly hugged each of their left ring fingers.

"The rings you gave us!" exclaimed Chasmira, staring at the sapphire glistening upon her hand.

"But I thought you said there were six—" began Krystal, but then Amanda Danielle drew from beneath her dress a chain hanging about her neck. Upon the gold strand glittered a diamond ring.

"One of us needs to get these stones to Aaron, but of course, the only way Rorrim will let us out of this room is by agreeing to give the stones to him. Our advantage is this—the stones can only be given up *willingly* by their destined owners. He cannot force them from us. However, I'm sure he has done his research, and I'm sure he knows something about what the stones look like, so we need some piece of jewelry that looks like one of our stones. We can present to him a false Summoning Stone. Then, perhaps, he'll let one of us roam a bit freer, thinking that person on his side, and we can figure out how to get the stones to the boys from there."

"What if he tries to *use* the fake stone?" asked Hailey.

"Well, I'm hoping he won't try to summon anything with it until he possesses more of the stones. Because, you see, if used one by one, they contain less energy than if used all at once. We'll just have to chance it, hoping and praying he waits. Now, does anyone have any jewels we can possibly use?"

Rachel held out her wrist. "You can use my bracelet. There's some kind of blue charms on it."

"They're shaped like *horses*, Rachel," Krystal pointed out. "I don't think Rorrim would be fooled *that* easily."

"Well, if they're all we've got—"

"Wait. My bracelet—the gems are amethyst like my ring."

"Uh-uh." Rachel shook her head. "Not the one Josh gave you—"

"Josh's life is at stake. And so are many other lives. Even if they *do* go nicely with my complexion, I'm willing to give them up for a greater purpose. Besides, I think I should go anyhow. You, Chasmira, and Hailey are all too close to Nathan, Aaron, Sam, and, well, maybe not Josh, but anyhow, I think I'd look least suspicious trying to give up my stone. Rorrim was our janitor long enough to know I never greatly favored Aaron or Josh to be too concerned with helping them. I mean, I'm sure he remembers all the spills he had to clean up from our pranking each other constantly..."

Amanda Danielle's eyes glittered as she listened intently and thoughtfully, beaming. "Wisely put, Miss Smith. The bracelet should work. Does anyone have anything else?"

No one else wore jewelry, so the plan's dependence rested upon Krystal's ability to fool Rorrim.

"Keep the real stone in your pocket," said Amanda Danielle. "Don't let him see it. Now, are you ready? It will be very risky, and you must quickly figure out a way we can get the stones to the boys."

Krystal nodded. "I know I can do it, Mrs. Daniels."

Amanda Danielle's smile was small but hopeful. "Then I have faith in you, and in Amiel, that He will protect and guide you. Come, let us all pray together first..."

After they prayed both for the boys' mission and their own, Krystal placed the bracelet containing the amethyst jewels in one pocket and slipped her ring containing the real summoning stone in the other.

Making her way to the door, she opened the small flap. "Excuse me, guard? I'd like to speak to Lord Rorrim. It's about the summoning stones."

"*Lord* Rorrim?" hissed Rachel. "Don't overdo it..."

As Amanda Danielle hushed her, the door slowly squeaked open. In the doorway appeared a tall, muscular, powerful looking soldier clad in black armor and wielding a huge spear. Krystal felt very small and shy as he commanded in a deep voice, "Come. I will take you to his tower." As she glanced back at the encouraging faces of her friends and Mrs. Daniels before the door shut on them, reassurance washed over the throbbing fear of her heart. Besides, there was no going back now. She must go through with this, or at least try, for all their sakes.

As the soldier led Krystal through the fortress, a strange hush clung to the place, not an eerie quiet so much, rather a gloomy, death-like sorrow. Krystal made certain to take in her surroundings. Perhaps they could prove helpful later on.

Finally, they reached the black door. The soldier opened it, shoved Krystal inside, and locked the door behind him. Krystal gulped. Rorrim sat on one side of the room at an ornate desk, mulling over some sort of paper. The thought of being locked in a room with Rorrim made her shiver, but she tried to mask her face with confident composure as he looked up.

"Ah," he mused, smiling slyly. "So glad to see you've come to your senses so quickly. Come here."

Krystal walked over, her heart gagging her voice. How did he know she came to offer one of the stones to him? She hoped he did not guess her treachery.

As she stood before Rorrim, he stared right into her eyes with a cool, emotionless glare. It was hard not to look away, yet it was the overwhelming fear itself which kept her eyes locked, terrified, upon his. Besides, she must show no signs of suspicion, reveal no possible dishonesty. Fear, yes, surely he expected that. But her gaze, however terrifed, must remain steady, true...

"And why do you choose to betray your friends by giving your stone to me?" he asked coolly.

"To be quite frankly honest, I'm quite tired of staying in that tower all day." Krystal tried to maintain a calm, collected, nonchalant appearance, though inwardly, she felt sick with fear. "I've come to give up my stone in exchange for the freedom to explore the castle. Besides, Mrs. Daniels says you can't do much harm without *all* the stones." She offered what she hoped proved a coyly triumphant smirk.

Rorrim's face seemed to darken at the mere mention of Amanda Danielle's name. His eyes flickered temptingly upon the bracelet, yet in his eyes too shone a doubt, a wariness. For a while, the debate ensued within those eyes, driving Krystal nearly mad as she wondered what he would do. What a struggle it was to hold her own gaze unwavering, trustworthy, sure of herself when she felt the entire opposite of all these things...

As Krystal held out the amethyst bracelet, Rorrim grinned slyly. "Very well. I shall exchange your stone for a bit of free reign. But how can I be sure this is the real stone?"

"Umm..." Krystal grew yet more uneasy, glancing away for one, painful second. Her reserve and quick wit rapidly escaped her.

"There is a way to prove it," he assured with deceitful calm. "All you need to do is reveal its power."

"It—its what?" Fear flashed plainly in her eyes now.

"Well, each stone has its own special power. I'm sure your Mrs. Daniels told you that, or is she not really so wise?"

Krystal felt a jab of anger. She couldn't let him insult Amanda Danielle, couldn't let him prove her treachery, and yet, what could she do? Did the stones really possess other powers besides summoning, or was Rorrim just trying to screw with her head?

"Of course she told us," Krystal found herself lying, though in a firm, confident voice, much to her surprise.

"Then reveal it. Reveal your stone's power."

"Umm..." Krystal was wishing very much that Amanda Danielle *did* tell her about some sort of special powers when a soldier barged into the room, exclaiming, "Sir, a message—"

"I m a bit busy, Gnarls—" Rorrim snarled.

"—about the enemy. Toby is helping them."

Rorrim blanched, unable to conceal his disgusted horror. The mention of this name seemed even more particularly revolting to him than Amanda Danielle's. He cast a warning glare at Krystal before leading Gnarls into an adjoining room.

Krystal took a deep breath. She had to think fast. Glancing about the room, her eyes fell upon a black onyx stone lying upon a small table. *It must be Rorrim's summoning stone.*

Glancing cautiously back at the doorway through which Rorrim and Gnarls exited, she slowly walked over and peered down at the rock. Upon the table also lay many scattered papers and open books, all about magical stones. Her eyes fell across one page that read, "In addition to having summoning powers, summoning stones each have their own individual powers. To find the stone's power, you must hold the stone and repeat these words; *lever ruory rewop*."

Her heart catapulting, Krystal shot another fast glance over her shoulder at the doorway, then reached into her pocket, pulling out her amethyst ring. Holding it in her palm, she quickly muttered the magic words. Nothing happened at first, but then one word appeared on the stone's surface. *Invisibility*.

"Invisibility?" she breathed. *It must be the stone's secret power, but how am I to use it?* Suddenly, footsteps approached, and as she whirled, her eyes widened as Rorrim and Gnarls entered.

She was caught now for sure. Rorrim would see her holding the real stone, and she would either have to give it up or he would send her back to her room empty-handed.

They stared right at her—no, not only at *her*, but all about the room in bewilderment.

"Where is she?" Rorrim growled.

"Maybe she—" began Gnarls, but Rorrim cut in.

"I locked the door when she entered the tower! *Now where could she have gone?*"

Krystal scarcely breathed, realizing she unlocked her stone's power simply by breathing the word. She was invisible! She still held a chance of escaping without Rorrim even getting her bracelet.

"Don't stand there gaping like an idiot!" Rorrim shouted to Gnarls. "Go sound an alert! Find the girl!"

Gnarls hurried out.

Walking to the large table that stood in the middle of the room, he beat his fist on it, snarling in frustration.

Then he wandered to the table where Krystal stood, and she quietly inched away.

He picked up the black onyx stone, stepped over to the window, flung it open, and held the stone out before him while shouting into the air, "I summon the twin dragons of the Ash Mountains!"

Dark wisps of shadow ringed the stone, as though it would've glowed with light if placed in more righteous hands. The shadows lengthened, spiraling out from the gem like ghostly tentacles. The room darkened, black clouds gathered outside, cruel lightning fingers curling from them. Krystal stifled a scream as two creatures shot from the clouds. Dragons, like long, black snakes with bat-like wings and cold, colorless, heartless eyes, hideous fangs and claws. Smoke rose from their nostrils, as if a fire constantly blazed in the pits of their stomachs. Slithering through the air, they flew up to the window. Krystal shuddered at the mere sight of their close proximity. Then Rorrim commanded in a loud, jarringly authoritative voice,

"Fly now to the Black Shores, where a ship approaches, and there destroy the four men who command the ship and any who may travel with them."

As they slinked off into the sky, screeching with terribly ominous promises to fulfill their new master's request, a new fear rose up in Krystal. She struggled to control her short, frightened breaths, glancing paranoid at Rorrim, whose eyes and ears thankfully focused solely upon the new catalysts of his destructive plan.

"Dear Lord," she prayed silently. "Help the boys defeat those dragons. Keep them safe. And help me use my new power to help them in any way I can. In Amiel's Name we ask this grace. Amen."

CHAPTER 9

The ship stopped of its own will a few feet from land. The boys departed, wading through the shallows to shore.

The island stretched shadowy and gray, like a cloudy day that never ends, coupled with the feeling of someone's dark eye is ever watching. Beyond the sandy beach scrolled a forest, but its great trees loomed completely gray and dead. It seemed no light penetrated the woods for many years.

Aaron spied a large object shadowed against a boulder some yards off.

"What's that?"

"I'll check it out." Nathan headed in that direction.

He returned huffing and puffing. "It's a small boat."

Aaron stared suspiciously. "Looks like we might have company. Everyone keep an eye out."

They shifted towards the woods. Up close, the trees were silvery black, broad, full of shadows, leafless and lifeless.

"Rorrim picks some cheery places, ehh?" mumbled Nathan.

Finding a place where the trees stood closely knitted, a half-way suitable hiding place, they set a small camp fire.

"So what's our status?" Aaron asked Sam as he rummaged about their packs.

"Three days' food and water, no map, no idea where we're going," he quipped, a bit too calmly in Aaron's opinion.

"Ahh, that's...comforting..."

"You won't get far that way," spoke a man's voice. Immediately, the four boys sprang up, brandishing swords, turning in the direction the voice floated from.

From the shadows stepped a tall form, cloak and hood concealing all physical features except for his striking, blue eyes.

"Who are you?" Aaron demanded.

As the man drew back his hood, the boys jumped at the startling sight. One side of his face was disfigured, appearing badly burned at one time, but his other features, including those of the other, whole half of his face, looked very handsome, even kingly. He possessed a strong jaw yet a smooth, boyish face. The firelight glinting upon his hair shimmered with every color of the spectrum. He held Aaron's eyes with a strong, commanding and unwavering gaze.

"I am Tobias of the Prismatic people, called Toby by friends."

"And are we your friends?" Aaron asked.

"Yes. In fact, you must take me as a friend whether you want to or not, for you cannot cross the desert without knowing its secret ways. Rorrim's fortress lies in the midst of a desert—the Desert of Endless Nights. The outer part of the desert is a wasteland, always covered by darkness. No light ever shines there. By day, it is blanketed by black clouds and fog. No wind stirs. The heat is stifling, the air heavy and humid, weighing down on you like a thousand hot hands pushing you down. The sand is black, scorching to touch. Not even the thickest boots can protect your feet from its wrath, and you will find no food, water, or shelter either. At night, the skies are clear of the fog but black and starless, save one star that still hangs over the fortress, barely shining like some frail thing on its deathbed, clinging to one last shred of hope. We call that star 'Eopo,' the last hope. It is the only thing that can guide you through the inner part of the desert once you've passed the wasteland."

"And why should we trust someone who knows so much about Rorrim's domain? How do we know you are not one of his men?"

Toby revealed a shimmering, gold pendant bearing the symbol of the dove and rose, just like those Amanda Danielle granted to them.

"Is this proof enough?"

"Yes." Aaron nodded. "Then...Amanda Danielle...are you looking for her too?"

Toby's gaze suddenly drifted from that of Aaron's. As he stared at the fire, the gleam in his eyes hardened. Then, he winced as if he recalled some distant memory from the depths of those flames.

"Yes," he said finally, very solemnly. "I have been looking for her for over one thousand years..."

The boys stared at Toby for some moments, thoughts and questions racing through their minds. Their thoughts were interrupted, however, by a hideous screeching.

"We've been spotted!" shouted Toby. "Quench the fire!"

The boys rushed to pour water and dirt on the flames. In an instant, it was nearly pitch black and deathly silent.

Without any warning, something descended rapidly, knocking Aaron and Nathan to the ground. The boys looked up. Two hideous, black dragons circled in the sky, bearing the most lethal claws and teeth the boys ever witnessed, glinting a visibly cruel white despite the darkness enshrouding them.

With lightning speed, they both dove for a fresh attack. Toby was ready, shooting two light arrows at once. They soared in different directions, each hitting one of the dragons who let fly heart-shattering screeches.

Quickly recovering from their shock, the boys banned together, swords drawn. The dragons swooped down again, this time knocking the swords from their hands, while Toby landed another shot with his bow.

"You won't defeat them like that," he shouted over the horrible cries. "They're too strong. We need to strategize. Spread out and use your bows."

Spreading out was the last thing they wanted to do, but it worked. They each claimed a different tree to circle and dodge behind. Of course, each dragon could only pursue one of them at a time, so while two of the boys distracted the dragons, the other two, along with Toby, tried to get in some good shots. The dragons shrieked each time a blow landed, and while they proved swift and challenging, after a while, they began to look ragged. And angry.

"Alright, Aaron, this is it." Toby bounded towards a tree on his left. "You take right, and I'll take left."

Aaron focused on his prey. The two dragons circled in rage then used their last ounce of strength to dive at him and Toby.

As they each released a final arrow, the beams of light struck the dragons. The boys watched in awe as the dragons writhed, screamed a last, hideous screech, and exploded right before their eyes. When the smoke cleared, no sign of the dragons lay in sight, not even a claw or a scale.

After they all caught their breath, Toby turned to the boys. "You fight well. Come, let us rest and eat."

"We don't have much food," reminded Sam.

"Don't worry about that. I have a replenishing bag. Replenishes any food I pull from it instantly. Let me put your food in there as well."

They all handed their food to him, figuring they may as well trust him. After all, he just risked his life to help them slay the two fiercest dragons they ever encountered.

"So." After they all ate a bit, Aaron looked up at him curiously. "Were you going to tell us how you know Amanda Danielle?"

"Yes." Toby's eyes flashed with deep seriousness, yet a small, amused smile tugged at his lips. "It all started when..."

* * *

As soon as Rorrim departed from his room to aid in the search for Krystal, she fled back to the tower. Finding one guard asleep and the other absent, she managed to snatch the keys and sneak through the door.

The other four girls, as well as Amanda Danielle, stared as the door opened and closed, seemingly on its own.

"Visibility!" Krystal whispered, suddenly standing before them.

Immediately, she was showered with questions, and when Krystal was finally able to explain herself, Amanda Danielle said, "I apologize, Krystal. I should've thought of the stones' special abilities. But this is good. We still have all the stones."

Krystal nodded then exclaimed, "Oh! I almost forgot. There was something else Gnarls said. He said some guy named 'Toby' was helping them. That didn't make Rorrim too happy—"

Krystal stopped, and they all jumped as something shattered on the floor. It was one of the cups Amanda Danielle materialized for them that morning. She dropped it and wore a very bewildered expression.

"Toby..." she whispered, gasping as if merely breathing became suddenly difficult. "It cannot be..."

"Mrs. Daniels?" Rachel frowned as they all stared at her, concerned and perplexed.

"Mrs. Daniels," Chasmira echoed, lightly touching her arm. Amanda Danielle shivered, snapping out of her reverie.

"Mrs. Daniels, who is Toby?" asked Hailey.

"He was...a long time ago...my fiancée..."

Again, they all stared, completely forgetting about their mission of getting the stones to the boys.

"Jiminy cricket..." breathed Rachel.

"But how?" asked Krystal. "And when—?"

"If I tell you," Amanda Danielle said in a low voice, "you must speak of it to no one—at least not until all these troubles are put behind us."

Nodding enthusiastically, they all waited eagerly for her to continue.

"It started over one thousand years ago..."

CHAPTER 10

"Mandy! Mandy!"

Gwendolyn's long, golden locks streamed behind her like sunrays as she rushed down the hallway to the sitting room. The young, Scintillate princess waved an envelope sealed with the emblem of a white dove.

"Another letter!"

"Calm down, child," laughed Eliot. He reigned as the current king of Iridescence, father of Amanda Danielle, Elisha, and Gwendolyn. His head was gray and his once-muscular figure thinner than in years past. His health waned for some months now. Yet a merry sparkle still shone in his eye as he glanced at Char, his beautiful wife who sat knitting, as well as each of his children. The excited Gwendolyn, his youngest; the youthful, handsome Elisha who sat engrossed in a book; finally his eldest, Amanda Danielle, who just turned sixteen, having grown into an elegant, refined, Amielian lady. She too sat knitting, but both she and Char looked up as Gwendolyn entered breathlessly.

Gwendolyn handed the letter to Amanda, chiming anxiously, "Do you think it's another invitation? Oh, open it! Read it!"

"Alright, alright." Amanda laughed lightly at her sister's enthusiasm.

She broke the seal and pulled the parchment out. Unfolding it, she read aloud, "*To Her Most Honorable Highness, the Lady Amanda—*"

"Ooo, how elegant," sighed Gwendolyn. Her eyes sparkled dreamily as though the letter was her own.

"*—the noble king of Prismatic invites you to his grand kingdom in the north where he will be hosting a magnificent masquerade. He shall be choosing his bride from those who attend.*

"*Please send your reply as soon as possible.*

"*Sincerely,*

"*Rorrim, High King of the Prismatic Isle.*"

As Amanda placed the letter back in the envelope, Eliot beamed. "Oh, how marvelous! Rorrim's father was a dear friend of mine, a great Amielian gentleman. I've heard good things about his son. I'm sure his father raised him in the ways of the Lord..."

Silence ensued as Eliot drifted into a state of thought, and Amanda studied him before asking quietly, "Do you think I should go, Papa?"

"Yes, child. No harm can come from it. I have a good feeling about this letter. Perhaps you will finally meet the one Amiel intends for you—"

Eliot burst into a coughing fit. Char rushed to his side, eyes gleaming with hurt, restrained tears. But he held up his hand, and as the coughing subsided, added, "No, my dear. I'm fine. Children, it's getting late. Why don't you go on up to bed..."

"Yes, Papa."

Each of them arose, and kissing first their father then their mother, quietly slipped from the room.

"Can I see your letter, Mandy?" asked Gwendolyn.

"Sure. But please give it back in the morning."

Gwendolyn skipped the rest of the way to her room, staring in delight at the shining seal on the envelope, while Elisha continued to his room, still reading and perfectly rounding the corner into his room at the same time.

So many thoughts swirled in Amanda's mind as she walked to her room. This would be the third ball she attended in the past month. Mama must soon depart for the Mira Vale, once father was gone, though she didn't like to think about that. Father wished to see her married to a good Amielian man. It was his last request. He yearned for the reassurance that she would be well taken care of, that a just ruler would sit on the throne beside her. At times, Amanda wished things could continue on as they were, allowing herself to remain innocently lost in writing her beloved poetry, playing the piano, singing, and spending precious time with her friends and family. She still felt too young and ill-equipped to inherit the responsibilities of wife, queen, and mother. But she loved her father dearly and was willing to make sacrifices to see his last wish fulfilled. Besides, her people would need a strong and able king once he passed.

She knew her father would want her to marry only a dedicated Amielian man. Of this, she was glad and in full agreement with, yet she still troubled over making the right choice, over finding the man Amiel would desire her to spend the rest of her days with.

So, kneeling beside her bed, she prayed only for one thing for herself. If Amiel would lead her to the sincere Amielian man He wished her to marry, she could learn to love him and be content, whoever he might be.

CHAPTER 11

Over one hundred young girls flocked to the palace the night before the ball. They were to spend the night in the palace's guest rooms. Over two hundred guest rooms occupied the palace, so there were plenty of rooms to spare for the princesses, heiresses, and all the other young, rich, or famous ladies invited.

Finally, the anticipated night arrived and all the princesses filed in, escorted by knights or other nobles bearing some impressive rank. As their names were announced, each descended the wide, winding staircase slowly and gracefully.

Rorrim sat on his throne, somewhat bored and unimpressed by the whole ceremony, when he suddenly looked up and sat very alert, his gaze glued to a slim, elegant figure just stepping off the staircase. She wore a sparkling, white dress with a full skirt and long, lacy, bell sleeves hanging off her shoulders. Her long, tightly spiraled curls were pulled back on the sides and clasped by diamond hair clips shaped like flowers. Diamond chandelier earrings hung down on either side of her rosy cheeks, diamonds strung about her neck, and a glittering white mask circled her blue-green eyes.

"Who is that?" said Rorrim lowly to Gustaff, his most trusted knight, who stood nearby.

"Who?" Gustaff's attention also strayed in his boredom, but now he followed Rorrim's gaze. "Ahh, her. Amanda Danielle, princess of Iridescence of Loz, heir to the throne, the most beautiful, and if I may mention, the richest heiress in all Zephyr's Islands. A good pick, my lord. It can't be long before her father, the king, dies, and then you would be king of Loz, the center of Zephyr's Islands. You would hold a great deal of power in your hands. Many would have to bow to you as king."

"Yes..." Rorrim muttered absently, his gaze particularly drawn to the emerald pendant dangling right below her string of diamonds.

As soon as all the princesses arrived, their presence announced, the dancing began. Rorrim already made his choice, but he would dance with some of the other ladies first, out of courtesy.

Meanwhile, Amanda Danielle stood by one of the tall columns, leaning against it as she watched the whirling couples. These balls always made her nervous, and she noticed the handsome king scrutinizing her carefully beneath his black, feathery mask. She jumped as someone said behind her, "Excuse me, but are you alright?"

As she turned, at first she thought it was the king, for his hair held every color of the rainbow, and thus he too was a pure Prismatic. But he was more simply dressed and wore a white mask on only half his face, the other half of which showed him to be quite handsome. Most alluring of all were his sapphire eyes; both could be seen, for the mask contained a small hole just large enough for his eye to peer through. Blushing vividly as his gaze met hers, Amanda Danielle looked away.

"Yes, sir, I just—I'm a bit dizzy."

"Would you like to go onto the balcony where we could get some fresh air?"

His voice was so quiet and gentle she felt much more at ease. Looking up into his beautiful, sapphire eyes, she smiled. "Yes, I should like that."

Offering his arm, he led her to the balcony. She stood gulping the air, feeling somewhat awkward as he stood silently—and handsomely—beside her. Yet his eyes didn't watch her hungrily like the king's. Rather, they reflected a deep pensiveness as they surveyed the stars, and interest soon replaced much of her anxiety.

After a few moments, the young man asked, "Are you feeling better?"

"Yes, quite. Thank you, sir."

"You're quite welcome. But forgive me. We've not been properly introduced. I am Tobias Daniels, chief musician and composer of the Prismatic Palace."

"I am Amanda Danielle, from Iridescence."

"An honor to meet you, Miss Amanda."

"And you, Mr. Daniels."

"Please..." Tobias smiled warmly. "You may call me Toby."

Amanda Danielle returned the smile. "Alright then, Toby."

Toby's gaze drifted to the emerald about her neck.

"That's a beautiful stone," he reflected.

"Thank you. It was a gift from my mother."

"I've never seen such a stone—triangular in shape—"

"Toby, my good man, what are you doing out here?"

It was Rorrim, the king. Amanda Danielle again felt herself blushing and looking away as soon as his dark eyes intensely met hers.

"I was just assisting this young lady," Toby replied. "She was dizzy and needed fresh air."

"And who is this lovely lady?"

"This is Amanda Danielle. She's come all the way from Iridescence."

"Really? An honor to meet you, my lady." He reached for her hand and kissed it. "Would you care for a dance?"

"Yes, my lord," she replied timidly.

Rorrim danced with her for a long time, and as they began to talk, she felt more comfortable, despite his eyes which did not decrease in their intensity. He asked her how she enjoyed occupying her time, and she told him of her interest in poetry and music. He complimented her beauty and mannerisms, wondering if she would sing for him and his guests. She agreed to, and while Toby played upon the piano, she sang. Everyone gazed in awe upon the small, angelic creature, especially Rorrim. Talented, beautiful, poised, rich—surely she would pose as the perfect trophy beside him. Meanwhile, Toby's gaze did not stray from her as he played the piano ever more softly, allowing her voice to resonate all the more clearly.

After she sang, Rorrim introduced her to Isabel, his younger sister, a lovely, bright, cheerful soul who was simply ecstatic about all the guests and excitement. She must've mentioned at least a half dozen times how much she enjoyed Amanda Danielle's singing, and Amanda liked her at once for her chipper spirit.

As the night drew to a close, the last dance arrived. This would be *the* dance, the final moment when Rorrim would choose his bride and reveal her by taking off her mask.

And, of course, to the shock of practically no one, Rorrim chose for his partner Amanda Danielle, the strangely quiet, exotic, blonde angel. They danced in the midst of the ballroom while everyone else stood aside, some brooding, some admiring. Then, as they stopped, Rorrim gently removed her mask, as well as his own, and announced that this was whom he chose to be his bride, if she agreed. Rorrim's charming mannerisms, gentleness, and intelligence more than convinced her. This was a man who could lead her kingdom, whom she could learn to love, and she consented. Cheers erupted in celebration of the engagement, though Toby watched on with solemnity clouding his eyes. Amanda Danielle caught that glance for just a second but then threw herself back into a state of complete bliss as everyone rushed forward to congratulate the newly engaged couple.

* * *

Amanda Danielle paused in her story to reflect. Then she sighed deeply. "If only I knew then of the conversation between Rorrim and Gustaff. Now that I look back, how could I have been deceived by such a selfish man? If I had known, I would have left that night, and yet Amiel planned everything perfectly as always, for if I left then, I would have never met...him..."

CHAPTER 12

Amanda Danielle spent a good deal of time with Rorrim over the following days. She sang, recited her poetry, or took walks with him in the garden. He bought her lavish gifts—clothes and jewelry, books and sheet music—and was always quick to compliment her and make her blush. A certain calm, cool, suave air clung to him, surging her heart into a mad twitter whenever he graced her presence.

Having written to her father, Father wrote back saying he was pleased with the match, having personally known Rorrim's father, a good Amielian gentleman. He heard good things about Rorrim too, both of his leadership as king and in his faithfulness. Father thought he must be a good Amielian gentleman just like his father, but he still wanted her to pray about it.

Amanda Danielle somewhat ignored this last bit of information though. She felt elated. How could any man be more taken with her than Rorrim, and how could she be more captivated by any man than him? What remained for her to debate or wonder over?

Then Rorrim announced he must go away for two weeks to attend to some business in another kingdom, while Amanda Danielle remained at his palace.

One day, as she knelt praying in the chapel, a voice broke into her thoughts,

"Excuse me, child."

She glanced up to see Pastyre Andrew, a kindly old man, approaching.

"Good morning, Pastyre Andrew," Amanda Danielle greeted, smiling affectionately.

"How is our soon-to-be-queen this lovely morning?"

"Very well, thank you."

A pause passed before Pastyre Andrew asked quietly, "Child, can I ask you something?"

"Yes, Father."

"Are you sure...are you *sure* you're making the right decision in marrying Rorrim?"

Amanda Danielle stared, surprised by this question. "Of course. He's a good man, and it's the best thing to do for my people."

"Have you prayed fervently about this, child? Do you know if it is right in your heart? Do you know if it is the Lord's will?"

Amanda grew uneasy and silent. She never really prayed about it. Though her original attitude was to find the sincere, Amielian husband Amiel knew was best for her, she quickly forgot that purpose. But then, Rorrim was a gentleman, and he *did* attend church services regularly. That had to count for something, didn't it?

Though she didn't acknowledge it before, her conscience bothered her, yet she argued against it, avoiding the reverend's question entirely as she insisted, "Rorrim respects and loves me, and I him. He has been very good and kind to me."

"And also very flattering?"

"Rorrim loves me," Amanda Danielle retorted firmly, though, for a moment, she wondered if she truly tried to convince her own self.

"And is it really Rorrim you love, or just a shadow of what you think he is and what you wish him to be?"

"Are you saying I shouldn't marry Rorrim?" Amanda snapped, though she looked away guiltily.

"I'm just saying that marriage is not to be entered into lightly. I'm saying you need to pray about it and make sure you're doing the right thing, child. I know your father wants to see you married, and I know your kingdom needs a king when he passes, but if you need more time to make your decision, I know your father would agree—he would not want you to do anything against Amiel's will."

An awkward silence passed between them. Amanda Danielle did not look up at the reverend but finally arose and said coolly, "Thank you, Pastyre Andrew, for your time and council."

She turned to leave but stopped and turned as Pastyre Andrew added, "Remember, child…man looks at the outward appearance, but our Lord God Amiel looks within the heart—as should we."

Amanda nodded curtly then continued down the hallway. She wasn't just looking on the outside, she told herself stubbornly—or was she? She didn't really know Rorrim. While she saw no proof that he wasn't a good Amielian, she possessed no proof he *was* either. And did he really love her as he always claimed? Father always taught them that love was more than words. Love was action. Rorrim had been gone for two days and still he did not send word as promised.

I will give it time, she told herself. She would give it time. And pray.

CHAPTER 13

Suddenly, the letters began appearing.

Every day she found a letter on her dresser. The letters were so different from the way Rorrim ever spoke to her before. Most significant was the content of the letter. It was more romantic, more sincere, more loving than anything she heard from Rorrim's actual lips so far. The words flowed like poetic waves, speaking of his appreciation of her heart, soul, and spirit, not just her outer beauty, voice, and talent, such as his normal compliments dictated. He began to sign the letters, 'From your Beloved,' and for a moment, she doubted if they actually came from Rorrim, especially when the roses and romantic sheet music started to arrive. And yet, who else could send them? Only royal family members could use the royal seal, and she knew Isabel would never devise such a prank. So her doubt about Rorrim began to lift as she fell deeper and deeper in love with the writer, beginning to write back.

* * *

It was very dark and silent as Amanda walked down the corridor towards her room one night. A cool breeze blew through the few arched windows left open, and her soft cream and sage green silks fluttered about her like a fair, feathery meadow, reminding her of fairies and butterflies and all the other dreamy visions floating about her head as of late.

Turning the corner, she stopped abruptly. She'd entered the hall with many paintings, and at the far end, a gleaming light approached. Amanda slipped back around the corner before cautiously peering around.

To her surprise, Isabel stepped into view at the far end of the hall. The light emanated from the candle she carried, and her eyes darted curiously about. She set the candle down beside the suit of armor standing next to the painting of the shepherd boy, and then did a most peculiar thing. Reaching inside the helmet and feeling around, she pulled something out, smiling gleefully as her eyes danced.

Amanda emerged from hiding. "Isabel? What are you doing?"

Isabel turned and gasped, her expression holding that of a shocked child just caught sneaking candy. Upon seeing only Amanda treading down the hall, though, she sighed, relief flooding her face.

"Oh, Mandy, it's you," she whispered, eyes lighting excitedly once more. "Come over quickly."

Amanda quickened her step, sure to make no noise, feeling that Isabel preferred whatever she was doing to remain very secretive. Upon reaching Isabel, she saw the thing she held in her hand. A letter.

"What is that?" Amanda asked curiously.

Isabel's eyes shifted somewhat nervously about the hallway. "Can you keep a secret?"

Amanda nodded.

Giving a short, satisfied nod in reply, Isabel returned, "But not here. Follow me."

Amanda followed Isabel down a few hallways to her room, and when they entered, Isabel quickly shut the door behind them, locking the door, as well as her window.

Then she sat on her bed and Amanda beside her.

Isabel's eyes implored Amanda's with a powerful, warning flare. "You promise to tell no one?"

"I give you my word," Amanda uttered quietly, exhilaration bubbling inside her at the thought of the secret mystery Isabel prepared to unfold before her.

The dreamy look in Isabel's eyes brightened, her elated expression returning as she spoke in rapid, hushed tones, "I've been receiving letters in the suit of armor ever since I was ten. It started with a letter I found in my room, but we—the writer and I—agreed to move the location to the suit of armor. The writer says it's more secret and safe. I just go there every so often and find them there, and then I leave my own letters in return, and in the morning, they're gone."

Amanda smiled too, looking down shyly. "I have been receiving notes as well."

Isabel's eyes nearly doubled in size. "Really?"

Amanda nodded. "And gifts."

"How are yours signed?"

"They aren't, except sometimes 'From your Beloved.' But I know they're from Rorrim. I've been getting them ever since he went away on his trip. He must be sending them from Spectrum. How I long for his return..."

As Amanda smiled dreamily, Isabel sighed, eyes turning stormily downcast. "I know *mine* aren't from Rorrim..."

"Who are yours from?"

"I don't know. They're always signed, 'With love, from your Secret Friend.'"

"May I see?"

"Certainly." Isabel handed Amanda the letter. "Sometimes, I think they're from an angel. The words are always so good and kind. At other times, I think perhaps one of the servants sends them, seeing my loneliness in this place. Rorrim won't let me actually *talk* to the servants. He says it's beneath one of royal lineage, which I know isn't true, but I don't like to anger him, so I just stick to writing the letters. It seems safer that way. Anyhow, whoever the writer is, I thank Amiel for sending me such a true friend..."

Isabel rattled on, but Amanda's thoughts suddenly drowned out Isabel's words as she turned the envelope over. It was enclosed with a white dove seal, just like the letters from Rorrim—or maybe not from Rorrim? Of course, anyone in the palace could've used the same seal, she told herself, if they were bold enough to get their hands on it. And perhaps Isabel was wrong. Maybe her letters really came from Rorrim too. Yet as Amanda opened it, unfolding the parchment, her hands quivered as she beheld those same, elegant letters and words— that same handwriting—as she caught a phrase of its contents— "I hear your brother is getting married to a beautiful Scintillate lady..." Her heart seemed to stop, and the note fell from her shaking hands, gliding to the floor.

"...though I wish I could see him face to face, just once—Mandy? Mandy, are you alright?"

Amanda realized she stared with wide eyes, as though beholding some horrifying ghost, and jolting back into reality, she picked up the letter. "Yes, yes, everything's fine..."

"Well, then, what does he say?" Isabel asked anxiously.

Amanda skimmed the last few lines and stammered, "Umm...he—it says he'll play you a new lullaby at ten o'clock?" She finished with a perplexed frown.

"Ahh, that's the best part," Isabel sighed. "Every night, I hear him playing music somewhere inside the castle. It's almost like he's hiding inside the walls, playing for me. He's a great composer, but we call his songs 'my lullabies...'"

Isabel's voice trailed off as the sound of some melody drifted towards them. It sounded like a violin playing; the tune was soft, distant, barely audible, but in the silence of the night, they could hear its gentle strain clearly.

Stretching herself out on the bed, Isabel listened intently, resting her chin in cupped hands, and Amanda did the same. The music was so peaceful that Amanda forgot her present worries. Following suit after Isabel, she soon drifted into a peaceful sleep.

CHAPTER 14

When Amanda awoke, it was not morning yet, only midnight. The music had ceased, and in the absence of its distraction, her troubles returned. She could understand some secret admirer befriending Isabel, but why herself? No, it wasn't really the letters which bothered her, but their words, and the roses, and that romantic song. Some other, invisible entity vied for her love. What if this person—if it even *was* a person—proved a threat, a danger? And how did he enter her own room unnoticed to drop off the letters, and when?

Suddenly, the music started again, only with a different tune. Always a naturally curious person, she quickly became very determined to delve to the bottom of this mystery. Very carefully, she crept from the bed where Isabel still slept with a contented smile upon her face.

Amanda walked all about the room, leaning close to the walls and listening, deciding the sound was closest near the wall next to the door. She felt along the wall carefully and her hand crept across something—a latch. There was a secret panel—her own castle held many like it—and it slid open easily without a sound.

She slipped inside and closed the panel, but not all the way in case she should need to return by that path. It was very dark within—barely any light penetrated—but she felt her way along the walls, following the music.

As she turned a corner, a dim light radiated up ahead. Treading down the narrow corridor, she turned then found herself at a dead end. On her right stood a door illuminated by a lantern shining above.

Amanda took down the lantern, slowly opened the door, and then peered out. As she looked out from the doorway, she gasped. On the left stood the suit of armor—she was in the painting hall, right where the picture of the shepherd boy should be, and she realized the door *was* the painting.

Obviously, the music did not float from that direction, so she stepped back and closed the door. But the next question was where to go next. The music was louder now, closer than when she began.

Pressing her ear against the wall, she fell through.

As she stood and looked behind her, holding up the lantern, she saw herself standing on the other side of the wall. She reached out and touched it. How very soft. It was some kind of curtain made to look exactly like a stone wall.

Continuing down the narrow corridor, the music pulsed steadily louder. It was getting quite loud when she reached another dead end. She used the lantern to shed light around the area and felt all along the walls. They were all real, no curtains this time. But then she noticed a stone that appeared slightly extended, and as she pushed it, the wall before her scrolled to the side. It was really a door that receded sideways.

Behind the door, a narrow, winding staircase spiraled upward, and using the lantern to light the way, she began the ascent.

As she climbed higher, her heart beat faster and faster, and she began to doubt her decision. What if her secret admirer really *was* a very dangerous person? Why would anyone keep themselves so secretive? Yet something drew her in. Whether sheer, childish curiosity or some greater, odd urgency, she wasn't certain, but the invisible, unknown force lured her upward and onward.

Finally, she reached a door. The music flowed very clearly now. Setting the lantern on a hook on the wall, she reached for the door handle, hand trembling. Taking a deep breath, she opened it.

To her surprise, however, only more darkness met her. As she opened it further, she saw pants, shirts, and other garments hanging, boots scattered on the floor. She entered someone's wardrobe, a gentleman's, by the looks of things.

Softly, deftly, barely daring to breathe, she crept forward, opened the wardrobe door a crack—for strangely there were handles *inside* the wardrobe—and peered through.

She was in a small but very finely furnished room hosting a canopy bed, a desk and chair, all ornately carved, and a tall, arched window. Amanda determined this must be one of the towers, for it looked small, round, and she climbed all those stairs to reach it.

On both floor and furniture lay scattered, musical instruments of all sorts, a couple music stands, and on the desk, stacks of paper piled very high, though very neatly.

Amanda's gaze, however, drew to the window, or rather, the person sitting on the window seat before the window. It was a man, and though he faced away from her, she could tell he was full Prismatic. His hair glistened in the candle light with every color of the rainbow.

Stepping forward slightly, in hopes to get a better view of him, she tripped over the boots and tumbled out of the wardrobe, crying out.

The man leapt from his seat, startled. As Amanda turned to look up at him, frightened of his reaction, she gasped. It was Tobias—the young, handsome,

Prismatic gentleman from the masquerade. She stared in shock, but also because almost the entire left side of his face looked as though it was once badly burned. He quickly turned and reached for something on the desk—a mask, the same he wore at the ball—when Amanda felt ashamed of herself for ogling so and urged, "No, please, wait. It's alright."

His hand paused over the mask, but he did not look at her.

"Did anyone follow you?" He spoke quietly, no anger singed his voice.

"No, Toby, I—"

"Are you sure—?"

"Yes, there was no one."

He sighed. "And now you know why we could never see each other again." He said it softly, as if to himself, yet she heard clearly and watched as he picked up the mask. This time, she did not try to stop him as the intense pain and sadness pooled in his eyes. Tears filled her own eyes as a great sense of compassion washed over her, as a strange urge to do anything to wipe away the hurt swelled within her.

The mask secured, he turned to her and offered his hand.

"Are you alright?"

"Yes, I'm fine," she replied softly, taking his hand and he helped her up. Rising, she searched his eyes, the deep waves of undulating sadness piercing her heart like cold waves, especially when he still did not look directly at her.

After leading her to the window seat, he sat in the chair at the desk.

"How did you find this place?"

"I followed the music."

"Why?"

"Because it was so beautiful. And I wanted to know who's been leaving me such lovely notes and gifts."

"It was Rorrim's orders," Tobias said quickly. "You see, I'm the royal composer, as well as the royal writer. Rorrim's been gone, so he asked me to leave you the gifts. He's never courted before—never had time to—and thought it would be better if I wrote the letters. Of course, he told me what he wanted put in them."

"You are a very elegant writer, sir, and a marvelous composer as well."

He smiled a little.

An awkward silence passed between them. So many comforting words she wanted to breathe, yet shyness overcame. Besides, the words she offered could in no way match the grandeur of those he wrote to her.

"Look, morning's in a few hours," he said finally. "Perhaps it's best if I take you back."

Amanda Danielle nodded.

This time, they did not use the secret passages, though Toby moved very slowly and peered cautiously around each corner before proceeding.

Finally, they stood in Amanda Danielle's room.

"Thank you, Toby. When can I see you again?"

Toby hesitated, a war of caution and desire and intense longing waging in his eyes.

"You can come to my room anytime. Just one thing—you must tell no one, and you must never be caught."

Amanda Danielle nodded. Then he bid her good-night and slipped stealthily out of sight.

CHAPTER 15

Amanda Danielle returned to his room every night. He shared his music with her, and she, in turn, told him much of her life at home and about her family. She asked about his own family, but on this subject he seemed very uncomfortable. When he only muttered that he *had* no family, she decided to leave the matter alone. If he wanted to talk, he would. Until he was ready, she would not pry.

As the weeks passed, Amanda Danielle and Toby grew to be close friends, and she eventually convinced him to remove the mask in her presence. The burn wasn't so bad. He was still very handsome, more so than Rorrim...

She stopped herself at this thought. Was she falling in love with Toby? She couldn't be. She loved Rorrim, and she must marry him, for her kingdom's sake.

However, one thing remained certain. Though she did not notice the way he looked at and smiled at her at first, *Toby* was quickly developing feelings beyond friendship for *her*.

Finally, one night, he said, "Mandy, there's something I must tell you that I should've told you before. And now that we're friends, it's been weighing upon me to tell you...who I really am."

"Go on," she said gently.

Toby took a deep breath. "I am...my brother is...I'm the prince of Prismatic. Isabel is my sister, and Rorrim my brother."

"Your *brother?*" She stared at Toby, her features no longer understanding but cold. This was the last thing she expected him to reveal. "You—you said you were the royal composer—"

"I am, but I'm also—look, I was just trying to protect you—"

"So you *lied?* You hid the truth?" She turned away, shaking her head in frustration.

"Yes, and I see now that all lies are wrong, whether meant for good or evil, but I *must* tell you the truth now. I cannot stand by and watch you marry a man such as Rorrim without knowing the truth." He growled these last words, disdain edging his voice as if uttering any part of this secret truth was the last thing he wished to do, and yet, it was so dreadfully necessary...

71

Slowly, she turned to him, the fire in her eyes somewhat relinquished, and she cast him a questioning look.

"I thought perhaps he really loved you, that there had been some change," he added, "but now I know...it would be better if you never married at all—"

"Rorrim *does* love me," she snapped, though she herself had come to doubt it.

"All he loves is that thing around your neck." Upon seeing her startled expression, he added more calmly, "Mandy, during the night of the ball, I heard Rorrim talking to Gustaff, his Chief Knight. Rorrim only wants to marry you for your inheritance—and for that stone you wear..."

"My stone? But why?"

"He seems to think it holds some power. Mandy, please trust me—let me explain..."

Amanda sighed. "Toby, please...just let me go back to my room. I have to pray...and think..."

* * *

Amanda Danielle trekked slowly and quietly down the dark hallways to her room, pondering carefully all Toby revealed to her.

She heaved a great sigh before entering her room and closing the door behind her. A click reverberated—the door locked—but she stood lost deep in thought, and the sound echoed distant and insignificant in her mind.

Amanda Danielle walked over to her chest with the mirror and reached out to turn on the lantern sitting there, when she noticed the shadowy outline of some person behind her. She opened her mouth to scream, but the person reached out and thrust a hand over her mouth. Her arms flailed, and the lantern knocked to the ground, the glass shattering, the light extinguished.

Another arm clutched her waist, and she kicked and struggled against the person who held her. But as he pinned her against the wall and she found herself staring up into his face, her eyes grew wide in shock.

"Rorrim?" she gasped, after he freed her mouth.

A wild flash of anger rippled in his eyes as he hissed, "Where have you been? Where did you go?"

"I—nowhere—went for a walk," Amanda Danielle stammered, suddenly frightened. She never saw Rorrim angry, upset or even annoyed. For the first time, she comprehended his great height and strength as he towered over her, holding her arms firmly in his large hands.

"Don't you lie to me!" he snarled, shaking her. "I know you've been to see *him!*" He spat the word "him" with unimaginable contempt and hatred, eyes flaring with the unpredictable, hardly controlled madness of a rabid dog.

"No, Rorrim, it's not like that—I asked him to teach me about music, I—"

"If you make any attempt to see him again, you will deeply regret it. *Do you understand me?*"

Amanda Danielle nodded. It was all she could do in her state of great fear and shock. Rorrim stormed from the room, slamming the door behind him. As Amanda Danielle rubbed her arms where Rorrim grabbed them, one thing flashed certainly in Amanda Danielle's mind. She would not listen to Rorrim but go back and listen to what Toby had been trying to tell her.

After waiting a while to make sure Rorrim must be sufficiently long gone, she slipped down to Isabel's room. Isabel still lay fast asleep, and so Amanda Danielle slipped easily through the secret door, closing it completely behind her.

CHAPTER 16

"I'm glad you came back." Toby took her hand, led her to the window seat, and together they sat. Deeply searching her eyes, he said, "What I'm about to tell you, you must tell no one."

"I promise."

He took a deep breath then let it out slowly. "When I was young, there was a fire in the palace. My mother died trying to save me. I was only two years old, and I hardly remember...but I *do* remember, somehow, Rorrim glaring—he was ten—glaring as though nothing was more frustrating than the fact that I still lived.

"He always hated me, jealous of the attention mother gave me. But when my father still loved me, despite the distorted face the fire gave me, my brother became all the more enraged, full of hate and spite.

"When I turned five, father remarried, and Isabel was born. I remember her big, blue eyes smiling up at me as she giggled in that tiny, childish voice. She was so small and innocent...

"But when she was two, both Father and my step-mother died—another fire. Young as I was, I surmised that neither of the fires were accidents...

"At fifteen, Rorrim took the Prismatic throne. He immediately shut me away in the tower, commanding everyone in the castle that no one was to speak of me as his brother. If I tried to see my sister or tell anyone who I was, Rorrim said he would harm Isabel, and she was the one and only person I still really loved, and so I remained in seclusion.

"For many years, no one spoke to me. The only human contact I had was with the servants who brought me food, clothes—Rorrim let me have whatever I needed or wanted, provided I keep in hiding. He did not know I used my monthly salary to gradually build a secret chamber beneath the castle—my Chamber of Music, I call it, where I often sneak away to compose, to be away from the room made my prison. Rorrim did not know all the secret passages I found, nor does he still.

"Despite my loneliness, there was one special friend that Amiel sent to me—Pastyre Andrew. He visited every Sunday and taught me about Amiel's everlasting love He has for everyone. I accepted Amiel as my Savior and made Him King of my life, and though I've felt lonely many a time, I can remember the verse, 'And lo, I am with you always,' and then thank Amiel for always staying right beside me, strengthening me.

"I began to turn from my hateful thoughts that I formed against my brother, and I began to pray for him. I still do. I know if it was not for Pastyre Andrew's guidance and Amiel's love and salvation within my heart, I might've turned out just as bitter and hateful towards my brother as he is towards me.

"I've tried witnessing to him these past years, but he only laughs. He is arrogant, thinking he needs only himself, that he can rule his life and decide his own fate, but I fear he shall find himself very lonely someday...

"As I grew older, Rorrim made the mask for me and said I could come out of my room on occasion, provided I wear the mask and call myself the castle's new, royal composer. I especially enjoyed the masquerades. As much as he detested it, I could talk to people, make a few friends, play my violin freely. But of course, it is our people's custom to hold masquerades, and they would certainly expect it from their king, so he felt obligated to host them, even if it proved in my benefit.

"And thus it has continued ever since..."

Amanda Danielle placed a hand on his arm. "Toby, I'm so sorry...and I'm sorry I didn't listen before. I did not see because...I did not *wish* to see..."

Softly caressing her face, he whispered, "It's alright..." He sat gazing into her eyes tenderly and with overwhelming, reassuring forgiveness before declaring, "Come. You have tarried here too long already. We must return before Rorrim notices you missing again."

CHAPTER 17

Toby had been telling the boys the same story from his own point of view. "I composed a song that night after she returned to her room, 'Mandy's Nocturne,' I called it. I wanted to play it for her in person, so I took my chances and left my tower, heading for her room.

"I practically skipped down the stairs as I hummed the melody reflecting her enchanting beauty. Moonlight streamed from the window, and I imagined her dancing, swathed in its beams like a mystical fairy princess. But as I headed down the hallway, a dim golden light approached, and I silently sank back into a doorway, covered in shadows, listening.

"The light grew steadily brighter as it neared, and yet it seemed to flicker. *It must be a candle*, I thought. Holding my breath as two forms passed the doorway and stopped only a couple feet beyond, I slowly turned my gaze in that direction.

"The two figures were Rorrim and Gustaff, and it was he who held the candle.

"I had to listen carefully, for they spoke lowly, quickly, and constantly glanced about as persons do when they are devising wicked plans.

"'Wait fifteen minutes,' said Rorrim. 'That should give me plenty of time to be in my room and in bed. But do not let yourself be seen. Once the job is done, dispose of this in my brother's room—' I caught the glint of a dagger as Rorrim handed it to Gustaff who hid it beneath his cloak. '—and after it is found there, the people will blame him for her death, and he will be disposed of, his ugly, staring mug finally off my hands for good.'

"Gustaff studied Rorrim seriously and asked, 'Are you sure you want me to do this?'

"'Yes,' Rorrim hissed coldly. 'I will not let that stone out of my grasp, nor will I allow her to humiliate me by breaking off the engagement. Besides, it's worth it just to get rid of that fool brother of mine. I should have done it long ago,' he added spitefully, and the words cut me like the knife Gustaff wielded. But I remained still as Rorrim said, 'Now, you know what to do?'

"'Yes, my lord.'

"'Then do not fail me.'

"'Yes, my lord.'

"'Oh, and Gustaff?'

"He turned back. 'Yes, my lord?'

"'I understand what a waste you consider it. If you like, you may indulge in a bit of fun with her for me before finishing the job. Just keep your fun to a minimum volume.'

"'Yes, my lord,' he added with greedy pleasure, eyes gleaming so hungrily I wanted to lunge and rip out his throat.

"But I flattened myself as much as I could against the wall as Rorrim passed the doorway and walked down the hallway. Then the candle's light vanished as Gustaff puffed it out, and I stood immersed in sudden darkness, like an ominous sign of the plot that lay in Rorrim's dark heart.

"Though both furious and hurt by my brother's words, I could not dwell upon that now. I must think of Mandy and her safety—her life. I could not see if Gustaff left the hallway yet or not, but he must not get into Amanda's room before I did. To be safe, I would take the secret passage to the second floor.

"As quietly and quickly as possible, I fled back to my room and donned my sword in case I should need it, though I silently prayed things would not have to come to that.

"By candle-light, I crept inside my wardrobe, opened a secret doorway, and hurried down the stairs, as well as a few corridors, until I reached a door.

"Extinguishing the candle, I slowly opened the door and peered out. No one seemed to be about, so I emerged from the shepherd boy painting and shut it behind me. I was not far from Mandy's room. But as I turned the corner, I could see a dim, golden light approaching. In only a couple minutes, Gustaff would round the other corner, bearing his steel blade.

"I hurried to Mandy's room. She sat on the sill of her window, windows thrown wide open, innocently reading. She looked up as I entered, gasping, and then sighed with relief as she saw who it was.

"'Mandy, listen to me,' I said, talking as softly as I could. 'You can't stay here. Rorrim means to kill you. Someone's on his way right now—I just overheard. You'll be caught if you go out that window...'

"I could see how much the words pained her. She already knew of Rorrim's wicked heart, but it is quite a blow to find out someone you love or loved can't wait to see you dead. I understood some of her pain, and it hurt me deeply to watch the wounds reflected on her face.

"But there was no time to trouble over these things. I said, 'I know a place where we can hide. No one else knows of it—we'll be safe there.'

"She nodded. Taking her hand, I led her hurriedly through a door which led to her sitting room, and then, to her shock, through a secret doorway in the back of the fireplace, which thankfully was not lit. As we fled down the corridor, we could hear Gustaff shouting in disgust as he found Mandy's room empty. I saw Mandy glance back fearfully, but I shut the secret door, praying it would remain closed.

"The hallway branched off, and we took the right-most path, which seemed to lead to a dead end, and the flaring torch on the wall seemed to be the only thing in sight. But then I pressed the secret switch—a stone in the ceiling—and the entire wall, as well as part of the floor, began to rotate, until we faced a different hallway leading to a large staircase lit brightly by torches. After treading down the steps and passing through another door, we stood in a huge room, and Amanda gasped, bewildered.

"On one side stood a pipe organ and grand piano, both beautifully crafted. Scattered about were loads of instruments, music stands, papers, desks, a chest, canopy bed, costumes, paintings, and lots of other wonderful and interesting pieces of artistry.

"'This is your Chamber of Music!' she cried, still whispering.

"'Yes,' I said. 'And it's safe here—only I and a few of my servants know of its whereabouts...'

"'Toby?' she said quietly. 'I'm sorry I didn't believe you before. All that you said about Rorrim...'

"'Shh,' I said softly. 'I understand.' Then I noticed how tired she was. 'Come,' I said. 'You should get some rest.'

"I led her over to the bed, and she laid down. As I turned to leave, she grabbed my hand and said, 'Toby?'

"'Yes?' I said.

"'Can you promise me something?'

"'Anything within my power, I will do.'

"'Then, promise me you'll never leave me, as long as we live.'

"'I promise.'

"She smiled dreamily and contentedly, then closed her eyes and drifted into what I hoped was a peaceful sleep. As I gazed wonderingly at her beauty, I thanked Amiel for such a true friend and asked Him to protect her, for she was the truest, greatest friend I ever knew besides Isabella. And I loved her. I loved her more than just a friend. I loved her as a man loves a woman whom he wishes someday will be his wife. As I prayed about this matter, I hoped deep in my heart she felt the same."

CHAPTER 18

After a good, long sleep, Amanda Danielle awoke. Many candles glowed, as well as torches running along the perimeter of the vast, almost cathedral-like room, their orange glimmer bouncing all about the walls, ceiling, and floor. Neither windows nor clocks stood in view, so she did not know the time, but as she sat up, she felt thoroughly awake and refreshed, thinking it must be morning.

Toby was nowhere in sight, and worry gripped her. But then she noted one of her dresses spread out on a chair, with a note pinned to it which read, "I've gone to fetch breakfast. I'll return soon, my love."

She smiled, and unpinning the note, sat it on the little table next to the bed. Drawing the curtain around the bed, she changed out of her nightgown, and into the dress Toby brought from her room during the night.

Sitting on the edge of the bed, she wondered what to do next. Her eyes wandered to the grand piano. It looked as though it was made of mahogany, and a wondrous sheen shimmered upon its smooth curves. Her fingers longed to play it, but she did not know if their hideout was completely soundproof. However, it would be safe at least to take a closer look.

Walking over, she ran her hand over the smooth mahogany, admiring the glossy, ivory keys, when suddenly—

"Mandy?"

She jumped, whirling. Toby stood before her with a large basket in hand.

"Toby." She sighed, smiling. "I wasn't going to play it. I just wanted to get a closer look."

"It's alright. And the place is soundproofed from most of the castle. Still, it might be wisest to keep as silent as possible for now."

He set the basket on the table and smiled. "Are you hungry?"

She returned a shy grin. "Yes, very much so."

They sat at the table, and after offering grace, Toby pulled from the basket two croissants, some cheese, bacon, and bottles of milk. Their meal continued silently until Amanda voiced the concern blazing in her mind.

"Toby, how are we going to get out of here?"

Toby sighed deeply. "Well, there are guards everywhere, so we'll never manage an escape on our own. I was nearly caught sneaking around this morning as it is. But there's another way. I still have servants that remain faithful to me but not to Rorrim. Actually, half the servants wouldn't be faithful to Rorrim if they weren't afraid of him. But I have talked to one of my most trusted servants, and he's going to send word to the Spectrum Isles—they're a nearby kingdom with whom we pledge alliance—and tell the queen there of Rorrim's deceit and cruelties. If all goes well, she will wage war against Rorrim, and with Rorrim distracted in battle, we'll have a chance to escape. Perhaps they'll even send some sort of rescue."

"But a war…Do you really want to put your people through such violance—just for us?"

"Not just for us." He shook his head. "But also for the people themselves. Don't you see? With Rorrim defeated, they can be free of his selfish, evil darkness forever. I think some of them know what kind of a man Rorrim *really* is. They know he's not the just, righteous king he would have the world believe. And also, remember your own people. If you were to marry Rorrim, he would become their king as well."

Amanda shuddered. "And where will we go once we've escaped?"

"We'll return to your homeland, in Iridescence. And there, I will fulfill my promise..."

He pulled from his pocket a glistening, white-gold chain, and strung upon it was the most elegant ring. She took in her breath. The band gleamed white-gold, carved with elegant filigree, and set in its midst was a large, glittering, white diamond, with two smaller diamonds flanking it. The gems glowed like tiny moon blossoms, their petals freshly unfurled. He set the chain around her neck, and she fingered it carefully as though it was the most delicate, beautiful treasure. And indeed, it *was* the greatest, save the look of love and admiration shimmering in his eyes as she gazed up into them.

* * *

Toby abruptly awoke Amanda Danielle the next morning.

"The Spectrum army is quickly approaching Rorrim's gates." Toby donned the sword with its sheath around his waist. "We must flee to my tower. The Spectrum people will provide us a way of escape from the window. Come—we must hurry."

He took her hand and led her to the door. But as he opened it, something sharp struck his arm, and he fell to the ground, stunned.

As Amanda Danielle looked up, she gasped. Standing in the doorway, glaring with a heartless, piercing gaze, was Rorrim, sword drawn, Toby's blood shining upon its tip.

Toby rose and stood before Amanda Danielle defensively, clutching his arm with one hand as the other inched towards his own sword. "How did you find us?"

"Do you take me for a fool, brother?" Rorrim snarled. "Do you think I didn't know you kept some secret place within this castle? The problem was finding it, but I obtained the necessary information from one of your servants. They're very loyal to you as I discovered, but not so loyal when tortured and their families threatened. And now I will take what is mine, do what I should've done long ago..."

Rorrim leapt from the doorway, swinging his sword as maniacal flames blazed in his eyes, but Toby quickly brandished his own blade and blocked the attack.

"It's over, Rorrim! Spectrum's armies are twice the size of yours and stronger!"

"That may be," he sneered. "But when I have gotten my revenge, as well as that stone, no armies will be able to stop me from ruling the world!"

"Rorrim, stop, *please!*" cried Amanda. "It doesn't have to be like this. You can take me prisoner, just don't hurt Toby!"

Their swords clashed and sparks sang as her pleas went ignored. But suddenly, Rorrim flipped Toby's sword out of his hands and Toby stumbled to the ground. Rorrim pointed his sword at Toby, and a sinister yet gleeful look gleamed in his eyes, such as that of a villain who finally attains his long-awaited dream.

"Give me the stone now, Amanda, and I will spare his life," Rorrim growled, though all the while glaring triumphantly at Toby who stared defiantly in return.

"I'll never give it to you," hissed Amanda.

"Well, then, say 'good-bye' to your lover—"

Rorrim's sword sliced down but it never hit Toby, for Amanda Danielle hefted Toby's fallen sword, blocking the blow. Rorrim's eyes scolding himself for his foolishness, he turned his fiery gaze upon her.

"Foolish girl," he hissed. "How can you love such a monster as him? Do you not see his face? Would you marry him instead of me, who offered you wealth, position—"

"You *deceived* me." Her eyes flashed with pure fire. "And I was foolish enough to fall for your smooth words. But your words are *poison*. He risked everything to offer his protection and love, and now I know who the *real* monster is!"

With that, she swung the sword, slashing a gash in Rorrim's side. He cried out in pain and surprise, stumbling to the ground.

Amanda helped Toby up, and taking sword in hand, he shouted, "Come on!" and led Amanda in a mad dash through the door and up the stairs. As they reached the crest of the steps, the door slammed down below—Rorrim managed to rise to his feet and pursued them.

"Hurry!"

On they flew until they emerged from the fireplace in Amanda Danielle's room. Toby and Amanda hastened to the hall with the shepherd boy painting and quickly crawled inside.

"Rorrim doesn't know this passage," said Toby. "We should get there before him."

Indeed, as they stepped into Toby's room, entering from the wardrobe, no one stood in sight.

Toby rushed to the window. "The battle has struck. But I don't see any sign of our rescue—"

Suddenly, a musical call wafted on the wind, and a golden phoenix speckled with ruby feathers swooped like a graceful cloud up to the window. Grabbing the iron bars in her talons, she jerked them right off the window.

"You go first," said Toby. "The phoenix is too young to carry more than one of us at a time."

"But Rorrim's coming—what if—? I don't want to leave you. I want to know that you'll be alright, that I'll see you again—"

Toby took her hand. "Mandy, everything will be alright. The phoenix will take you home. Go now to safety, Mandy, and I will come for you someday—I promise. Someday you shall stand in your tower and gaze out the window towards the east, and from there, you shall see me coming."

"Then I shall wait," she said softly, the tears choking back her words. She grasped the ring strung about her neck. "I shall wait..."

With that, she crawled out of the window onto the phoenix's back, and the bird soared away from the tower, high above the dangers of the battle raging below, the rising sun illuminating its wings with a fiery glow. All was madness beneath them, but the phoenix carried them high, enveloping Amanda with the high strides of its protective wings...

As Amanda glanced behind her, she stared and gasped in horror. Toby stood on the edge of the window, clashing swords with Rorrim, and then, suddenly, he toppled from the tower into the fires below.

"Turn around!" she shrieked. "We must go back! We must go back!"

But the phoenix would not turn, she must not disobey Toby's orders. Amanda Danielle wept bitterly as they flew off into the blood-red sunrise, the phoenix emitting a mournful wail reflecting the sharp shattering of Amanda Danielle's heart.

* * *

"That was the last I ever saw of Toby..." Amanda Danielle finished softly, sorrowfully, tears gently kissing her cheeks.

Tears streamed down each of the girls' faces as they cried silently, hearts flooded with compassion and sadness towards their beloved teacher.

Amanda Danielle's mind again wandered as she recalled one of her last memories of her father as well. It too was one of the most painful...

"I am sending you to the Mira Woods with your mother, child," he said. *"The Mira will build a safe haven for you there where no one can harm you. Elisha is young, but he is wise and strong for his age. He will take the throne. You will be safe with the Mira until the Hero comes to claim the stone."*

"And what if Toby comes for me?" she asked quietly, though she thought she knew the answer in her heart.

"Toby is dead, child..."

"I spent many lonely days in the garden. Of course, I had visitors, but I longed to see his face again, just once. But though I gazed from my tower into the east each day, he never came. Finally, I accepted the fact that he must be dead. A funeral was held in his honor, but I wasn't even allowed to go to say 'good-bye.' It was thought best, safest, that I stay in the garden. Finally, I decided that this was Amiel's will, and I knew I would never love another man like I did Toby. Yet, I was thankful to Amiel to have known him...I rededicated my life to Amiel and His service and eventually found Amiel wanted me to be a teacher. But now...if Toby is really alive after all these years..."

"Perhaps it was really meant to be." Chasmira placed a hand on Amanda Danielle's arm. "Only it wasn't the right timing. Amiel still had to prepare your hearts. Things only work out right if done in Amiel's timing, you always tell us that. Perhaps there is still hope."

A faint glimmer of a smile flickered in Amanda Danielle's eyes, touching her lips.

"Yes, there is always hope..."

"Tiffany?" Krystal's red-rimmed eyes darted about concernedly, almost frantically.

"Aww, man, of all times to just vanish," muttered Rachel.

"She does this all the time," Chasmira explained to Amanda Danielle. "But where could she have gone in Rorrim's fortress?"

"If she possesses the skill to slip from our grasp unnoticed, then I assure you she shall be quite fine," Amanda Danielle returned calmly, and as Rachel opened her mouth to retort, Amanda Danielle shook her head gently to silence her.

"As Miss Eriz has said, there is always hope. Even the most lost of souls are not completely lost unless they leave this world without finding the Light. So, until we die, and after for some, there is always hope. Everything will work out. I've a feeling about Tiffany. She'll be just fine..."

CHAPTER 19

"The first part of the desert is called the Outer Wastelands," explained Toby. "Its sands are black, so hot your feet cannot even touch them. The only way through is the secret cave beneath the Outer Wastelands. Its trials can prove perilous, but it's the only way to reach the Inner Wastelands where the sands, though also black, can be walked upon, and in the midst of the Inner Wastelands looms Rorrim's Castle..."

With this less-than-comforting thought, they started through the dead woods towards the desert.

After about an hour, the air grew steadily hotter. As their trek progressed, the heat became nearly unbearable, but then Toby turned and led them down a little hill to a single, large, solitary stone. He tapped the stone, and it slowly slid aside to reveal a large, dark, seemingly-endless hole.

"This is the way to the secret cave."

Josh gulped before muttering in a nervous tone, "Uhh...as I don't have my flying powers yet—and neither does Aaron—perhaps someone could fly me—er, us—down there."

"The hole is enshrouded in magical charms. The instant you enter it, you will lose flying powers for a time. The only way is straight down. Eventually, a wind will catch you and lead the rest of the way. Most people stop here and turn back out of fear. However, I warn you thus. This place tests your fears in ways you've never known. You can place your hope and faith of survival in nothing but the Lord Amiel. Only He may grant you strength to endure the following trials. Now, let us go."

Toby hopped in, looking far too comfortable about plunging into a random, endless black hole, in the boys' opinions. Aaron took a deep breath before taking that leap of faith, followed by Nathan then Sam, after first having to push Josh in.

They fell like rocks. Aaron could feel the wind rushing past at a discomforting, swift speed. Then, suddenly, a gust of air caught and carried him over a wide ravine to a ledge where Toby already stood, sheathed in a strange, orange, torchlight glow, granting him a more mysterious aura than usual.

Landing safely, the boys gathered around Toby. They noticed five doors—all plain, identical, and seemingly ordinary and harmless—were set in the wall behind them.

"What's with the doors?" asked Josh.

Toby explained, "This place is called the Hall of Truth. We must each pick a separate door. Through each door is a maze that will lead us each to the same room on the other side. However, I give you this warning. The walls are covered with mirrors. Do not look directly at the mirrors under any circumstance. They are made to show the deepest, inner-most fear of the person who looks into them, and many have gone mad by staring at and believing in their illusions. When you reach the end of the maze of mirrors, there should be a mirror shaped like an arched doorway. Walk straight through it, but do not look into the mirror."

"Alright. Are we all ready?"

The four boys nodded.

"Then let's go."

Together, they each stepped through a different doorway, and immediately, the doors slammed shut behind them.

* * *

As Tiffany delved deeper into the cave, a frosty cold began to settle upon her skin, the ice searing like fire. She'd wound through the cave a good hour now with no signs of the boys. She tread upon the wrong path, the one intended for them by another. At least his plan failed, at least the boys were safely where they should be. But then, where was the boy with the foiled plans...?

The further Tiffany traversed, the deeper the blue of the walls became, the colder it grew.

"This isn't right...I need to go back..."

But her own words echoed incomprehensibly in her ears. Her senses seemed numb. As she paused, a great sleepiness suddenly overtook her.

As she tried to take another step, she stumbled backwards, moaning as her head hit the wall, but a moment later, the sharp pain deadened, growing numb like everything else. She saw the blood dripping from her head to pool on the icy floor below, yet as she sunk to the ground, the blood blurred, everything blurred into a senseless mass of red and blue and white. Enough of her senses remained for her to think she was trapped, freezing to death. She called out weakly, hoping someone would hear...

* * *

Dristann sat at the cave's entrance, chin resting in the palm set upon his bended knee, brooding as stormily as the endless mass of gray clouds extending over the ocean. He had failed—again. Or did he ever really try? He knew his aunt's threats were idle—at least for now. Why should he help her? What did she ever give him? A self-centered enchantress for a mother, a woman just as full of malice, spite, a glutton for power like her sister. Neither of them gave a care for him, why should he...?

Raising his head, he strained his ears to listen. A distant, eerie cry, like the wind pleading for help, only this howl wasn't the wind. It was a girl urgently begging. He smiled wryly. Good. At least he did *something* right, after all...

No. Wait. He froze, rigid, suddenly wanting to vomit. No girls accompanied Aaron's gang. They were all secured in Rorrim's fortress. That meant—

He burst up, stumbling over his own feet as he surged through the caverns, calling her name frantically, abandoning his normal, graceful strides as he bounded through the cave, tripping in his panic, pushing back the cold as it quickly overwhelmed him...

Barging around a corner, there she lay, crumpled, blood frozen to her skin whose wonderful brown hue paled to a sickly blue. She struggled to turn her eyes upon him then closed them, shivering with that slightest exertion of strength.

Hefting her up—the sickening feeling gripped him tightly; how light and lifeless she floated in his arms—he whirled about, trying to decide—which way? He set the trap, he should know. This was not the time for his ignorance to overcome him. This was not the time for him to not care. He *must* care, about *her*, *for* her...

"Tiffany, wake up. We have to go back, you have to tell me which way..."

She moaned but did not stir. The sleepiness did not touch him, neither could the intense cold—his mother had been gracious enough to grant him such a gift, he thought scathingly. Yet if he didn't get her out of the cavern fast...

He ran. It was all he could do, run aimlessly, hoping to glance upon something familiar. Suddenly, he fell against the wall, and while he sat stunned, he didn't release his grasp on her. He slowly opened his eyes, but staring at the wall, it seemed he saw eyes staring back. His reflection? Perhaps the cold was great enough to make even him grow delirious. No. There were many pairs of eyes, all along the wall on either side. He blanched, holding back the vomit as he realized these were all real people—people who drifted down this same path, fell under the spell of the sleep and cold. They fell just as Tiffany into an endless sleep, freezing solid until they fused with the icy walls of their grave.

With renewed determination, Dristann sprang forward. Frost already settled upon Tiffany's brow. He could not allow her to be transformed into some icy statue, lonely, lost, forgotten, not after she rescued him from that same fate, if but for a vain time...

After several more panicked moments stretched before him like an over-whelming eternity, a light shone before him from the cave's entrance, a drab, dreary light, but in his eyes it blazed brilliantly as the sun with the hope it offered.

Surging into the island's sallow glow, he laid her on the hard ground, gazing down at her pale, blue face, his eyes tortured with the continued wonderment of not knowing what to do. He rescued her from the cave. Now what? How to save her from the pain? Perhaps he would leave her, someone would find her eventually, someone from the Council or perhaps even Aaron's motley gang...

He rose, hesitating, a pain splitting his heart as her brow furrowed, her lips moved, uttering incomprehensible syllables, her breath emitting in long, white, curling streamers as she shivered all over. Her fingers twitched, and then lifted just a bit. He had to turn, run *now*, or the will to do so would slip away. Taking a few steps back, still he faltered, still something gripped him to that spot, forced his eyes to behold her tortured face...

She lifted the trembling, frost-tipped fingers, grasping at the air, and the piti-fully pleading syllables took form, "Dris...Dris...tann. Dristann?"

His feet froze, rooted to the ground as if held steadfast by the same frost en-snaring her delicate body.

"Dristann...Dristann?" The cries intensified, heightening in volume and panic until she began to shake more violently, crying sweet tears that froze to her soft skin like shimmering diamonds. Those tears wrenched at his heart, shatter-ing it into millions of tiny fragments. How he desired for the ability to cry those tears for her...

Rushing to her side, he slipped the reaching hand into his own, shuddering, for the coldness of her touch outmatched his own. He stroked her icy forehead, massaged her icicle fingers until the blood began to pulse beneath the skin once more, 'til she began to wince from the pain of the returning sensation.

At last, she opened her eyes and breathed, "Were you really going to leave me?"

"My aunt...she expects me to help take down Aaron's crew," he muttered, trying to ignore the hurt blazing vividly in her eyes. He no longer possessed the strength to bear the pain of beholding her disappointment. His heart lay rent already, no longer capable of being whole.

"I don't think you put forth much of an effort," she whispered. "Considering they found the right cave anyways."

"It's *her* island. It's confusing."

"You know this place like the back of your hand. You visited here often as a child."

He scowled. "It's amazing how much you know, at times."

"Will you really leave me here, alone?" she whimpered, her tears threatening to break down the feeble wall of reserve yet forming its hardened shield around his heart, the one which so desired to feel for her yet couldn't, wasn't allowed to.

"I don't have a choice, do I?" he sneered. "You should know how furious she'll be if I just up and disappear, abandon her."

"Yet you would abandon the one who loves you, your best friend?" she pleaded more than questioned. "You know I cannot die. Nor can I sustain permanent injuries. But you would leave me to suffer the pain of my body returning to normal, possibly risk throwing me into some awful disease, for an aunt who doesn't know the meaning of being a good friend at all? Would you really leave me, Dristann?"

She sobbed, choking pitifully on his name as she lay immobile, save the tears which flowed as freely as the memory rushing back to him, slipping so easily, with steath over his heart's protective barriers...

He was eleven then, the first time she came to him, also as an eleven-year-old. He felt so special then, especially when she told him this wasn't even his own story, he wasn't even the main character. He was just an aside, yet she treasured him beyond all other characters. How honored he felt, a great respect and awe towards her developing in him rapidly, and with those feelings, a friendship. It was almost like having an imaginary friend, for she promised she was invisible to everyone but him. She made it so. This made him feel all the more sacred in her eyes.

Often he took her to his special place in the woods, away from the palace shrouded ever by shadows and shadowy, frightening guests. Deeper in the forest, the trees stretched tall, thin, and not quite so tight knit so that beams of sunlight filtered down like fairies dancing. When the mist scrolled through the light pillars, it was like the fairies sending them messages with their magic dust.

That's what she always said, that upon each pillar of light, a message was carried, a musical message, but you had to be a fairy to hear, or else an extremely good listener. He thought he heard one of the songs once...or perhaps it was just her quiet singing. She loved to sing, especially for him, and he loved to listen to her lilting voice, like a sweet angel's lyre...

How many times they would race through the trees, laughing, playing, carefree...that's how it always was with her, the reason he most relished her presence. For while she was there, it was as though no one else existed save the two of them. Nothing else mattered but her and the calm she brought him. Sometimes he even asked her to make him invisible for a little while so he could be like her, so nothing could harm him, neither magic nor hand nor the piercing stares of his mother and aunt.

Invisibility could not stave off his clumsiness though. He often received cuts, scrapes, and bruises on their ventures, the usual child-like stuff. But one day, he fell head-first down a long, sloping hill, rolling and rolling 'til a large tree stopped him sharply, the rough bark ripping a great gash in his flesh. She rushed down the hill, frantically calling his name, her voice piercing as his head throbbed, great rivers of blood matting in his hair, trickling over his eyes, staining his arm. It felt sticky in his hand, and he began to cry, the feel of the cold, slimy stuff frightening him as it gushed all over, but he couldn't move, his leg felt weird, smashed, contorted beneath his body...

But then she hovered over him like some celestial maiden from a fairy tale. She didn't return him to his mother, knowing she would be furious at his irresponsibility, knowing she might bestow the promised, dreaded "gift" upon him even sooner. No, instead, she closed her eyes, breathing one of her limited wishes just to heal his broken body, to clear the blood and pain and fear away...

How he wished he could bleed now, feel the pain coursing through her—feel it ten-fold if he had to—so that he might remove her undeserved torment. He would rather bleed to death to spare her, abandoning the smooth grace his mother's gift bestowed upon him. What did such grace profit him save to make this innocent being fall unhealthily in love with the worse person imaginable, the one man who could never be good enough for her nor good *for* her?

"Do you need my help here?" he asked. "Does Aaron need something I can do?"

"No," she sighed. "He will pass his trial...I only meant to make it easier for him..."

She gasped sharply, wincing in pain, her whole body tensing as feeling began to stab her skin all over like millions of tiny knives. He knew. That's how it felt, the deprivation...his tongue stung even now with the bitter tang of her blood wafting through the air...

He couldn't bear her pain any longer. He mustn't think about what he was about to do. He must do it, must release her pain, just as she once relieved his. Hefting her in his arms, he glided with the speed of spreading fire through the gloom of the woods towards the ocean.

* * *

Aaron found himself in a hall whose walls were covered from floor to ceiling with mirrors. As a shadow flashed in one of the long stretches of silvery glass, he instantly looked away, remembering Toby's warning.

Trying to keep his gaze focused on the floor, he started slowly down the path which soon curved to the right. He wanted to walk faster, or even run—a strange desire to leave this room as soon as possible gripped him—but he couldn't. It was all he could do to concentrate on not looking at the mirrors as some eerily possessive pull urged him to glimpse just one, tiny peek. He wished Toby gave them some warning about how difficult it would be to resist their temptation, though he wondered how or if the knowing would help him. He tried to keep the constant, watching eyes of the mirrors from his mind, but the longer he tread down that silent path with only his echoing footsteps to distract his mind, he began to ask himself... *What is my deepest, inner-most fear?*

Reaching a fork in the path, he veered left, hoping he was going the right way. All the while that single, troubling question repeated itself in his mind. *What is my greatest fear? My deepest terror? My secret-most horror? My...?*

His feet began to drag like lead, wanting to stop, and his eyes wanted to glance up and catch just a peep of whatever glimmered in those mirrors.

Abruptly, he stood at a dead end. *Good*, he thought, sighing great relief. *I must be at the end of the maze.* He tried to walk through the mirror as Toby said. But no matter how he pushed or ran into it, he couldn't get through.

Then he remembered the fork in the path. Perhaps he chose the wrong way and this wasn't the arched doorway. But instead of turning about and going back to try the other pathway, he looked up just to check...

Instantly, his eyes fixed on the mirror before him, and he could not tear away. Shadows, dark shadows, swirled in the mirror, and then a dark tower took form. The scene zoomed in on the tower's window. Inside were the girls and Rorrim who wielded a black staff. He suddenly grabbed Chasmira and threw her against the opposite wall. Aaron could see her fear-stricken, pleading eyes as Rorrim lifted his staff, pointed it straight at her heart. He saw her scream and could almost hear it as jets of black energy surged from Rorrim's staff straight towards Chasmira. Aaron found himself drawing his sword and shouting, "No!" Everything grew abruptly black. Then the mirror became a mirror again.

Aaron was relieved it stopped. It all seemed so real—*too* real. But now he knew what his greatest fear was. Though he never wanted to lose any of his friends, most of all, he felt terrified of losing his closest friend, Chasmira. And Rorrim knew it. He sent the visions to trouble Aaron. He captured Chasmira to use her as bait to bring Aaron to him, so he could find a way to take his stone and bring him to his downfall.

One, determined thought raced through Aaron's mind—he must get out of here as quickly as possible. He had to get to Chasmira. Rorrim couldn't harm her so long as she possessed her ring, but what if she tried to get it to them and failed? That was just the sort of thing she would try to do...

Shadows stirred in the mirror again. No, in *each* mirror. The scene was re-playing all around him. He tried to look away, but it surrounded him, playing over and over again—there was nowhere else to turn—each time more quickly culminating to the part where Rorrim aimed his staff at Chasmira...

Aaron clutched his sword tightly. His heart cavorted frantically within him, he was breathing heavily, and beads of sweat began to form thickly on his brow. Chasmira's eyes pleaded to him from all sides, yet he couldn't get to her, couldn't help her...

Toby's words pushed through the madness into the realm of his conscious...

"...many have gone mad staring at and believing in their illusions..." *It wasn't real*, he told himself. *If I really want to help Chasmira, I have to turn away...*

He made a sudden bolt down the hallway, stumbling against the walls as he went, the scene still playing all about him. As he approached the fork, he flung himself down the right path even as his own feet resisted, trying to betray him by keeping him captive. Racing as fast as he could, he soon skidded to a halt before a dead end. He looked up. It was the mirror shaped like an ached doorway, and yet, now he came to it, he could not go through. Chasmira's death played over and over on this mirror as well, larger and more realistic than ever. He wished only to get away from it—*please no, don't make me go forward*. But Amanda Danielle's words flashed in his mind... "...remember that Amiel is the Light of the world—He will be your Light when all other lights go out.

"And you must have courage. Courage is not being fearless. It is being willing to face and overcome your fears, because some things are more important than your fear, such as saving your friends—saving Chasmira..."

"Dear Amiel, help me get through this!" he cried, and then, with a last bit of strength and courage he knew came only from answered prayer, leapt through the mirror.

He landed somewhat ungracefully on the other side, falling to the ground, and yet he had made it. He lay thanking Amiel silently as Nathan, Sam, Josh, and Toby all crowded around him.

"Are you okay?" asked Toby, his voice grave.

"Yeah." Aaron sat up. He was still quite pale and shaking but felt much better away from the presence residing inside that room.

"You were in there a while," said Nathan. "We thought you'd—" He seemed about to say something like "We thought you'd croaked," but as his face contorted, perhaps he realized the insensitivity of these words and decided instead, "Umm, glad you made it."

"I'm sorry, everyone. I should've listened."

"Well, you'll be alright now," said Toby. "It must've taken a great deal of courage to face your greatest fear."

"I couldn't have done it without the Lord's help...or Amanda Danielle's encouragement."

"I'm sure the Lord is pleased with such faith in Him." Toby smiled. "And Mandy would be proud too.

"Come. We have a long way yet to go."

CHAPTER 20

"This stone's power is warping," explained Amanda Danielle. "This is how we will get the stones to the boys."

Amanda Danielle had been inspecting each of their stones. Now the girls watched her carefully examining Chasmira's sapphire and waited for her to continue.

"With this stone, you should be able to warp to the desert, give the five stones to the boys, and use it to warp back. Of course, the boys will have only six stones instead of seven, but Rorrim only possesses one, so their army will majorly outnumber his both in number and power. Here, Chasmira, put these in your pockets."

Amanda Danielle slipped the five stones, including her ring, into Chasmira's pockets, while returning her own stone.

"Are you ready?" Amanda Danielle asked. "We've no time to lose."

Chasmira nodded affirmatively.

"Then repeat after me. 'Warp to Aaron Ruiz in the Desert of Endless Nights.'"

Chasmira grasped the stone tightly.

"Warp to Aaron Ruiz in the Desert of Endless Nights."

Closing her eyes tight, she expected to be caught up in some great whirlwind, and when she landed, she felt the dry, stifling air of the desert surrounding her. But she felt nothing. Opening her eyes, she saw she yet stood in the tower, and Krystal, Rachel, Hailey, and, randomly—Tiff—all stared at her, looking just as confused.

"Mrs. Daniels?" Chasmira began, but as they all turned, she suddenly no longer stood beside them. Donning her diamond ring again, a thin stream of white light like a laser shot from it as she walked around the perimeter of the room, scanning the walls with the light beam. Finally, she pocketed the ring and rejoined the girls.

"It's as I thought," she sighed. "The room is sealed by a barrier that allows no one to warp from it. Rorrim must've guessed that one of the stones might be a warping stone."

"Then I'll just take it outside and warp with the other stones to where the boys are," said Krystal.

Amanda Danielle shook her head. "It's not that simple. You see, while anyone can use the stones to summon people and armies and such, only their guardians can use their special powers. Only Chasmira can use the stone to warp."

"We'll just trick Rorrim then, to get her out of the room—like Krystal did," suggested Rachel.

"But we don't have any more fake stones." Chasmira frowned. "And I don't think Rorrim is stupid enough to consider falling for another trick."

They all sighed, their great plan seemingly thwarted.

Then, quietly, Hailey said, "Why couldn't we *make* our own fake stones?"

Everyone turned and stared at her.

"And how do you expect us to make rocks?" Rachel snorted.

"No, it's not such a bad idea..." Amanda Danielle said slowly, her expression very pensive. "We *could* make stones—not summoning stones, but stones with the same powers as ours. When we gave them to Rorrim, he would ask us to reveal their power, only this time, we'd be able to. However, such magic is very complex, and all the necessary materials are probably packed up in some secret room of Rorrim's. Besides, if we all give him fake stones, he's likely to become suspicious of why we're so eager to help him. And with Krystal running loose, he might think it's a ploy for us to get free reign of the castle and escape. Rorrim's an intelligent man...we need another way to get the stones to the boys..."

As she reasoned this, she walked over to the window and gazed out at the vast stretch of gloomy desert. Then, her eyes strayed to the trees in the courtyard right below their window. She smiled a bit as a memory flashed in her mind, a memory of a night she and Toby spent in his room. He played his violin while she sat gazing down at the beautiful cherry blossoms. She imagined she could see those blossoms even now, though the trees were dull, dead, barren. But as she studied them more closely, a wonderful realization struck her. They were the same trees, nine trees in a circle, and she caught a glimpse of what looked like the remains of a broken fountain in their midst. It all came together now. They stood in Toby's room. They had been here the whole time, and now they were going to escape.

Amanda Danielle rushed to the wardrobe, thrusting the doors open wide. There was nothing inside, but the secret entrance was boarded up.

"Mrs. Daniels, what're you doing?" asked Chasmira as she and the other girls crowded around, wondering.

"Stand aside, girls." The girls inched back, though still peering at her curiously, and Amanda Danielle held out her hand which wore the ring. A ball of white light appeared in her hand, and she hurled it inside the wardrobe. A loud bang like an explosion boomed, and an opening gaped in the back of the wardrobe, revealing the passage.

The guard's voice boomed outside the room, "*Hey! What's going on in there?*"

"I'll keep him busy." Krystal turned herself invisible.

The other four girls hopped in the wardrobe, followed by Amanda Danielle who shut the wardrobe doors behind them. Tiffany used her healing stone to repair the hole blasted in the wardrobe.

As they scurried down the stairs, they could hear the guard barging into their room, shouting, "The prisoners! They've—" He stopped here and slouched to the ground, unconscious, for Krystal hit him over the head with a chair.

After several moments, she heard someone else rushing up the stairs to their room. She stood next to the door, chair poised and ready to swing, when she heard a voice say, "I tell you, Rorrim's got some new trick up his sleeve, some magical device. Says he'll find the stones for sure now..."

"Well, never mind that," said another voice with a thick, British accent. "Let's just see what Charlie's yellin' abou'."

Two guards entered, shocked expressions spreading across their faces.

"Blimey! What happened to ol' Charlie? And where are all the bloody prisoners—?"

Both guards suddenly slumped, knocked out on the floor. After throwing the chair down, Krystal rushed from the room towards Rorrim's tower. As risky as it was, Krystal knew she must find out more about this "new device" of Rorrim's. A feeling of knowing gripped her. If it had to do with him getting the stones, they could all be in even greater danger than they were already.

Meanwhile, Amanda Danielle led Chasmira, Rachel, Hailey, and Tiffany down the familiar corridors and stairways and finally into a huge, open room, the largest they'd ever seen.

"Is this it?" breathed Hailey as they stared at its vastness. "Is this the Chamber of Music?"

"Yes..." Amanda Danielle stood reminiscing, gazing at the great columns and archways. It was exactly like it was so many years ago, with the exception that Rorrim either removed or destroyed Toby's things long ago.

Snapping back into the present, Amanda Danielle turned to Chasmira. "Are you ready?"

"Yes."

"Alright then. We'll wait right here for you."

Chasmira nodded. Noticing the nervousness flickering in her eyes, Amanda Danielle added, "We'll be praying for you too."

With that final bit of encouragement, Chasmira held up the hand on which the sapphire rested, shouting, "To Aaron Ruiz in the Desert of Endless Nights!"

All at once, she felt as though she was spinning rapidly, her breath knocked out of her. She moved so fast that everything rushed by in a solid blur, and then that blur darkened and everything stopped. She was there, in the Desert of Endless Nights.

CHAPTER 21

Or rather, she stood in a tent. A soft, cool breeze blew in through the flap. A gleam of firelight also entered to land upon the figure that lay sleeping in the tent. It was Aaron. She softly crept over and sat beside him, watching him sleep for some moments. How peaceful he looked. His breathing rose and fell soft and steady. The dim firelight glinted upon his face and midnight black hair, illuminating his silver highlights. He looked not only peaceful but very handsome. Chasmira almost decided not to awaken him. She was sure that none of the boys had gotten much sleep lately. How tired he must be. Also, she did not wish to end her reverie, desiring the serene moment to stretch on. Realizing her own tiredness, she thought if only she could just curl up beside him...

Yet, much more important matters stood at hand, and so she softly called his name,

"Aaron...Aaron, wake up..."

CHAPTER 22

Aaron was lost in a wonderful dream. He and Chasmira walked in the moonlight through the garden. Leading her to their special place, they just sat together under the phoenix tree, gazing at the stars and talking of old times. Then they drifted to sleep under the tree together, but she must've awoken, for she was calling his name...

Aaron slowly opened his eyes. Chasmira's face smiled down at him. He must still be dreaming. Closing his eyes, he tried to force himself to go back to sleep, not wanting the dream to end. But the voice continued to call his name. Maybe he should get up. Perhaps it was really Toby calling him. Perhaps it was time to go, and, after all, the sooner they got going, the sooner he really *would* get to see Chasmira again, he hoped.

So as he opened his eyes again, his shock was so great that he bolted upright, staring.

"Chasmira?"

"Yes. I didn't mean to startle you—"

"Is it really you? I thought I was still dreaming!"

"Yes, it's me." She beamed at his thrilled reaction.

"How—?"

"No time to explain. I've brought five of the stones—well, I have six, but the one I need to warp back with—"

"Sure, come on!"

Aaron grabbed her hand and excitedly dragged her from the tent to where Toby sat by the fire.

Upon seeing them approach, Toby arose.

"And who have we here?"

"This is Chasmira, sir. She's brought six stones."

Toby's eyes lit up. "Praise be to Amiel! Aaron, go fetch the other boys."

As Aaron rushed off to the other tents, Toby gently took Chasmira's hand and kissed it. "An honor to meet you, Miss Chasmira."

Chasmira smiled, glad it was too dark for him to make out her intense blushing. "And you, sir. Amanda Danielle's told us all about you."

A wave of mingled exhilaration and anxiousness rippled in his eyes. "Mandy...how is she?"

"She's fine, we all are—"

"Like, wow! Aaron *wasn't* seeing things!"

Josh rushed over to greet Chasmira—Nathan, Sam and Aaron soon following—bombarding her with questions. Toby allowed Chasmira to answer a few before gently interrupting, "Come, there will be time for stories later. We must use the stones to summon the army which shall lead us, Amiel-willing, to our victory.

"We hold eight stones. We must divide them among ourselves."

"Eight?" echoed Chasmira.

"Yes. The six you've brought—"

"I need the one to warp back."

"Of course. We will use it to help summon the army, and then you can take it back with you. Also, we have Aaron's stone and my own."

He revealed a smooth, opal ring gleaming with a multi-colored sheen.

"You have it!" exclaimed Chasmira. "Amanda Danielle said there was another stone, but she didn't know where it disappeared too."

Toby nodded with a small smirk. "I have guarded it well these past years. Now, you, Aaron and I have our own stones. Perhaps you'd like to pass out the rest, Miss Chasmira?"

"Of course..."

She dug the rings containing the precious stones out of her pockets and carefully began handing them out, all the while talking excitedly.

"Here, Nathan, I'm sure Rachel would want you to have hers, and, Sam, here's Hailey's...

"Here, Josh. This is Krystal's amethyst. And I thought you might like Tiffany's aquamarine too."

Lastly, Chasmira approached Toby.

"Would you like to take Amanda Danielle's stone?" she asked with timid tenderness, holding out the ring.

Toby gazed down at the gem, and with a smile, closed her hand over it. "No. If she entrusted it to you, I'm sure she would want you to help summon the armies with it. Besides, I have my opal, and that satisfies me."

She shyly returned the smile as Toby led the six of them to encircle the fire.

"Alright," declared Toby. "Say, 'we summon the Armies of Light,' when I say—now!"

"We summon the Armies of Light!" they shouted into the darkness, Toby bearing his shimmering opal, Aaron holding up his blue topaz, Chasmira stretching forth the hand on which rested Amanda Danielle's diamond and her own sapphire, Nathan holding Rachel's blood-glowing ruby, Sam extending Hailey's glittering emerald, and Josh raising Krystal's amethyst and Tiffany's aquamarine high, like tiny but brilliant stars.

Nothing seemed to happen. All stood very calm and still.

"Where are they?" asked Nathan.

"Wait—I see something," whispering Sam, gazing into the west. By the dim light of the camp fire, the faint outline of a crowd of people stood before them.

"It's too dark still," said Toby. "We can't see them."

Chasmira remembered Amanda Danielle's diamond. It glowed a pale, milky white in the darkness, but as she read the words flashing upon it, she held it up and shouted, "Star beam, light the way!" Bright rays of light shot from the tiny stone, blinding them with its brilliance. The light pierced the black clouds, dispersing them and allowing the sun to shine through again, casting a celestial glow upon the helms of over 10,000 armed soldiers. Aaron, Chasmira, Toby, Nathan, Sam and Josh all stared with reverent, humbled awe upon the vast army standing at their command.

After recovering from some of their incredulity, Toby and Aaron marched up to the captain of the armies, a tall, proud, Prismatic man whose hair glittered many shades of purple, blue, and indigo. The soldiers' armor glistened like thousands of golden stars, and the crest of a white dove carrying the white lily was painted on their breastplates.

"Welcome, great Captain of Light," greeted Toby. "You are indeed a welcome sight in these times of need."

The Captain nodded. "As is the sun. We have been waiting a long time to bring peace back into this land and again reclaim it for the Prismatics. The sun is a sign of hope that such a longing will be fulfilled.

"I am Hallate, and here are my armies. We promise to serve you, even to death, for we know who you are, my lords. Hail to Tobias, rightful king of the Prismatic Isle! Hail to Aaron, the great Hero of 1,000 years! And hail to his companions, the Heroes of Light, of which many deeds are also known."

"Thank you, my good captain. Shall we now talk of our battle plans?"

"Yes, let us waste no time."

Hallate followed Toby and Aaron into the tent where Toby declared immediately, "I think we should ride out at once."

Hallate stared at him. "My lord?"

"Rorrim knows nothing of the lady Chasmira being here. Therefore, he does not know we have summoned you. Perhaps we may surprise him. We can reach his fortress by sunrise tomorrow."

"Surely he has spies, and will notice that the black clouds no longer rest over the desert—"

Toby pondered this fact for a moment. "This is true. But even if he *does* know of our coming, he will not be able to summon an army larger than 2,000, for he holds only one of the stones, and he has used some of its strength already in his haste. Don't you see—he cannot win. We can easily surround and overtake his fortress. He will have many foul beasts on his side—"

"But our men are strong, and we carry with us the powerful weapons of light forged by the Prismatics long ago," Hallate nodded, agreeing to the plan.

Toby then turned to Aaron. "Master Aaron, do you agree also?"

Aaron took a deep breath, staring down at the map, its lines and curves incomprehensible scribbles as his head swam. This was what they came for—to make war against Rorrim and defeat him. But now that the time dawned ever nearer, things seemed to happen so quickly. It was so surreal. He was going to lead an army of more than 10,000 into battle alongside a destined king and a renowned captain.

"Well, what are we waiting for?" he said at last.

"Good," smiled Hallate. "All we need to discuss now are the troops' positions—"

"Excuse me?" Chasmira's head appeared through the flap of the tent. "I'm very sorry to interrupt, but could I please speak with Aaron a few moments?"

"Could you please excuse me, Captain?" Aaron asked.

Hallate glanced at Chasmira, then Aaron, and with an understanding smile, nodded.

Aaron exited the tent and stood before Chasmira.

"I need to get going," she said. "The others will worry about me."

"I know. Thanks for everything."

She smiled slightly then added, very softly, "So...I guess this is it...the final battle..."

"Yep..."

"I—we'll be praying for you..."

A hint of worry flickered in her eyes. Taking her hand, he said confidently, "Hey, we'll all be fine. It's like Mrs. Daniels told me, 'Amiel is the Light of the world, and we need not fear the darkness if the Light shines in our hearts.' I believe Amiel will help us win this war."

"I just want to know...that I'll see you again..." She bit her lip, tears almost choking her last words.

"You will. You'll gaze out your tower, and you'll see me coming from the east."

Chasmira smiled. Then she set in his hand the diamond ring and closed his fingers around it.

"Here, I bequeath this ring and its power to you. May it protect you in this, your darkest trial."

Smiling reassuringly, he clutched it firmly. Then she took out her sapphire and, in a flash, was gone.

CHAPTER 23

Amanda Danielle, Tiffany, Rachel, and Hailey all waited patiently for Chasmira's return, praying all the while.

"Stop!" Krystal cried, bursting into the room.

"Krystal, what's wrong?" Amanda Danielle asked as they all stared at the troubled expression flooding Krystal's face.

"When did Chasmira leave?"

"About an hour ago—"

"Good," she mumbled to herself. "So he doesn't know yet..."

"Know what? Krystal, what's going on?" Amanda Danielle demanded, serious concern flaring in her voice.

"It's Rorrim. He's created a new device. It's a map. When one of the stones is used, it shows *where* it was used. That means—"

"When Chasmira returns, he'll know someone's been in the desert with one of the stones and has brought it back here," Amanda Danielle finished. "He might catch on to all of our plans. Did he say *why* he made the map?"

"He's looking for Aaron—knows he has one of the stones. His men haven't been able to locate him and the boys for days—"

In a bright flash, Chasmira returned, hers the only face beaming brightly.

"The boys are fine, and Toby's leading them, and now they've summoned a huge army to attack Rorrim—" She paused, her own expression turning stormily grave. "What's happened?"

"Rorrim knows about the stones," replied Amanda Danielle. "Quickly, hide the warp stone—"

Just as Chasmira slipped it into her pocket, the door burst open, and Rorrim stormed in. He clenched his black staff tightly in hand, so tightly the hand turned a stark white and red. Fierce rage furiously seared his eyes, the girls rendering frozen in fear save for their trembling bodies. Amanda Danielle looked on in a different kind of fear. She witnessed his wrath before and loathed now to see it again.

"Where are the stones, you vermin?" he snarled.

"And I don't mean this blasted thing!" He held up his hand, and Krystal's bracelet rested in his palm where it shattered into tiny pieces.

"Now, which of you will tell me where the *real* stones are before I kill all of you?"

He turned to Amanda Danielle. "*You.*" His voice oozed with pure malice and hatred. "You always did stand in my way."

Marching up to her, only a few inches separated his face from hers as he towered over her. "I'm sure you're the leader of all this. Now tell me what you've done with them."

But Amanda Danielle no longer quailed before him for a new strength and confidence filled her. Glaring defiantly, she hissed, "I no longer fear you. I fight for what is right, and I know that in the end, Amiel will grant us the victory...and *you* will fall."

They glared deeply into each other's eyes for a few, challenging moments. Then, with a sudden, quick blow, Rorrim struck Amanda Danielle upon the head with his staff and she fell to the ground, unconscious.

Anger rose up in the girls—especially Chasmira. Filled with such an incredible rage, she glowered at him with a before unknown fierceness. "*I* did it. *I* hid the stones in the desert, where you will *never* find them."

Rorrim struck a blow at Chasmira, but she quickly jumped out of the way. Hailey, Rachel, Tiff, and Krystal let out a shout and leapt at him, punching and kicking at him. In the end, they barely scratched him, and he threw them all against a wall. He might've killed them all right then when the distant call of a trumpet sounded, and a soldier rushed in to meet Rorrim.

"My, lord." He bowed his head.

"*Can't you see I'm busy?*" Rorrim shouted.

"The enemy has been spotted—on the ridge, only a few hundred yards from the castle."

"Are they alone?" Rorrim hissed.

"Yes, my lord, just the five of them."

"Good...take these prisoners back to their tower and guard them well. I will be along soon to...welcome our guests..." He cast another hateful glare at Chasmira, which she returned with a glare of her own.

The guards roughly grabbed the girls and dragged them back to their room. Rorrim sealed the wardrobe entrance with a powerful barrier, casting a final, defiant glance at Amanda Danielle as the guard laid her on the mattress closest to the window. Then his spiteful eye turned to Chasmira, that perfect, little, mirror image of Amanda. She propped her beloved teacher's head on a soft pillow that had been crammed in Hailey's backpack. As he whirled from the room, his eyes filled with a new hatred and determination.

CHAPTER 24

Chasmira gently stroked Amanda Danielle's soft curls.

"Any change?" whispered Rachel.

"No," sighed Chasmira. "She still hasn't awoken."

Yet as a ray of soft, golden sunlight streamed from the window, resting upon Amanda Danielle's face, she slowly opened her eyes.

"Wait," gasped Chasmira, "she's awakening."

Krystal, Hailey, Tiff, and Rachel rushed to Amanda Danielle's side, watching with hopeful excitement.

"The sun rises," she said softly, her eyes smiling drowsily, distantly as if beholding some afar, wondrous dream. "The darkness is no more. They are coming..."

"Who?" asked Chasmira. "Who's coming?"

"The Armies of Light, the Armies of the Sunrise. They are coming from the east, led by the true king. Come, let us go to the window."

As they helped her to her feet and over to the window, she sat upon the window seat. Clustering around her and gazing out the window, they took in their breath, overcome with awe.

As the sun rose, the first sunrise seen in Prismatic in many years, it crept over a distant, sandy ridge. Over that ridge also rose the greatest army they ever beheld, and at the head of that army stood Toby and Aaron and a strong Prismatic captain, flanked by Josh, Sam, and Nathan. Their armor glistened like millions of gold teardrops as the sun scintillated off of their breastplates and helms. As the sun ascended higher, the desert itself was changed, the sand beneath their feet no longer black but pure white and glistening like diamonds uncountable as the stars.

As the sun rose higher behind the great army, casting a celestial, majestic, mighty glow about them, the Prismatic captain blew his trumpet and the thousands of gold-clad soldiers charged over the ridge, down the hill towards Rorrim's castle.

Amanda Danielle smiled, the tears glistening in her eyes turned to liquid gold in the sun's warm glow. She breathed, "Our prayers have been answered."

The Armies of Light descended upon Rorrim's troops which seemed so small and insignificant next to the thousands of Toby's armies. As the battle ensued, Rachel exclaimed things like, "Whoa! Jikes! That's gonna leave a mark," and "Aww, *come on!* Man, Rorrim's soldiers are stupider than Rorrim himself..."

Krystal would've remarked that she didn't think "stupider" was a word but suddenly pointed and shouted, "Whoa, Josh just slugged some guy with his sword!"

Only moments later, someone busted down the door. It was Sam.

"Sammy!" cried Hailey.

"Come on," urged Sam. "Before more guards show up."

"Mrs. Daniels is hurt—" began Chasmira, but the great fairy arose. "I feel my hope renewed, and with it, my strength. I have strength enough to flee this place."

Sam hurried them down the winding steps. Bodies of dead or dying guards lay scattered where they won the bad fortune of encountering Sam. They rushed down another flight of steps but suddenly, someone appeared from around the corner, blocking their path.

Rorrim.

Sam slashed at him with his sword, knocking him to the ground. For a moment, Rorrim lay stunned or at least surprised by Sam's boldness, and they rushed past him. But as they raced down the hallway, Chasmira screamed as someone roughly grabbed her arm, yanking her close.

She struggled to get free, but Rorrim threw her against a wall, and she slouched to the floor, stunned. Sam and the girls rushed towards them, but Rorrim pointed the staff at Chasmira's heart, his eyes glinting dangerously, and they stopped short.

"Move a step closer, and I end her life," he snarled.

Then, in a blaze of blinding smoke and fire, both he and Chasmira vanished.

"Now what?" cried Rachel.

"You all need to get out of here," declared Sam. "I'll find Toby and tell him Chasmira's in trouble. Come on!"

CHAPTER 25

Aaron plunged thick into the fight. Many Shadowmen lay slain around him, while more continuously ensued.

Suddenly, a shadow flashed in his mind along with a vision of Chasmira. Something prodded him to look into the sky, and as he did, a dark cloud swirled about one of the towers. Within the cloud replayed the same scene he witnessed in the hall of truth, and Rorrim's voice hissed cruelly in his ear, "*I would come soon, Aaron Ruiz, before I take away from you your most precious thing... forever...*"

Aaron bolted towards the fortress, abruptly blind to everything else swirling about him. Rorrim wasn't messing with his head this time. This was not just some horrible dream or smoky illusion. Chasmira was in trouble.

Aaron stumbled in the midst of his sprint as Toby shouted, "Aaron, where are you going?"

"Chasmira's in trouble!"

Toby took a final swing at a hideous, goblin-like creature before bolting after him.

As they reached the fortress, Toby declared, "They're probably in Rorrim's tower. I'll lead the way."

* * *

Rorrim held Chasmira in one arm. Struggle as she might, his strength was unfathomable, and he held her firmly in his grasp.

Someone burst into the room, sword wielded, ferocity blazing defiantly upon his face.

"Aaron!" cried Chasmira.

Rorrim clutched Chasmira closer with one arm while pointing the staff at Chasmira's heart with the other.

"Let her go, Rorrim," Aaron growled.

"I don't think so," sneered Rorrim. "Unless we can come to some sort of... compromise..."

Aaron raised his head slightly. "I'm listening."

"You command your Armies of Light to cease fighting," hissed Rorrim, "or I will obliterate your friend."

It sounded more like a threat than a compromise, in Aaron's opinion. But he would agree to appease Rorrim. He had nothing to worry about. Toby would enter any moment from the secret door.

"Alright."

"Aaron, don't do it!" Chasmira cried. "Don't listen to him!"

Aaron knew she was trying to be brave, yet at the same time, her eyes fearfully pleaded to save her, to choose her. Her mind willed him to defy Rorrim's proposal, but her eyes revealed her heart's cry...Why didn't Toby hurry? Her gaze was pure torture...

Someone leapt up behind Rorrim, grabbing the arm that held the staff and pressing a sharp blade against his neck.

"Ahh, Toby," jeered Rorrim. "Back from the dead. How cheery—"

"Release the girl," Toby growled lowly, a dangerous look glinting in his eyes, the tone of his voice utterly serious and threatening.

"Surely you wouldn't kill your own brother. You don't have the guts."

"Don't tempt me, Rorrim," Toby hissed, and for a moment, they caught each other's eye.

"Fine," decided Rorrim, releasing Chasmira who rushed to Aaron's side. Toby released Rorrim but did not sheath his sword.

"I will let you all go. However, if I am to stay up in my tower and die—" His eyes flashed cold and emotionless at first, but then a spiteful glint flared in them. "—then you shall all die with me."

With that, he struck the floor with his staff. The whole castle shook with ominous tremors, chunks of rock beginning to rain down from the ceiling. Aaron, Chasmira, and Toby all leapt out of the way as the rocks plummeted towards them.

When the dust cleared, Rorrim had vanished, but spotting the tip of his cape as he disappeared through the doorway, Toby bolted towards his brother, commanding, "Aaron, take Chasmira to safety while you still can!"

Toby hurried down the winding stairs, crashing against walls as the tower shook violently, and he struggled to dodge falling debris.

He followed Rorrim out of the tower, down several corridors. Toby knew where Rorrim was going. He headed for Toby's tower, the room that was once his home—and his prison.

Toby almost lost sight of Rorrim several times, but the tip of his cape flowing as he slipped around corners led him.

Finally, Toby made it to the shepherd's painting. Surprised to see it still hanging after so many years, he jumped inside, scurried down the familiar passage, and then bounded up the spiral stairs. He flung himself from the wardrobe, sword ready, but saw no one.

Then a cape was thrown over his face from behind, momentarily blinding him as his sword was knocked from his hand. Toby spun around to break free and found himself standing before the tower window. On the far side of the room, Rorrim glared menacingly, maliciously, hatefully, aiming the tip of his black staff right at Toby's heart.

Toby returned the challenging glare, not glancing away for an instant.

"Well, well, well," Rorrim mocked. "Doesn't this look familiar? Again you stand before me defenseless, only this time, you will *not* get away…

"Obliterate!"

As Rorrim shouted the word, a black jet of swirling, lightning-fast shadows shot from the staff, but they never touched Toby. He shouted, "Materialize!" at the same time, and one of the light army's shields appeared in his hand. The attack did not bounce off his shield though. The shield seemed rather to absorb the attack's power.

Rorrim stood taken aback for a moment by the materialization of the shield and the realization that his brother yet stood before him whole, intact. He forgot that Toby wielded one of the rings. As Toby blocked a second shot from his staff, the shield began glowing an even brighter shade of gold.

"You fool, why don't you give up?" Rorrim hissed. "Once I knock that ring from your hand, there will be no hope for you, and you cannot kill me while I wear my own ring."

"That's true." Toby blocked a third attack, the shield gleaming brighter than ever. "But everyone possesses at least one weakness, and there is one way to defeat a summoning stone bearer—use his own attack against him! Shield of Light, release your power!"

All the energy the shield absorbed erupted from it, converted from dark energy into white light. The pure, brilliant streams pierced Rorrim's body like a thousand knives, and then, in a surprisingly swift flash, he vanished forever. All that remained was his staff which fell at Toby's feet, its hollow form echoing as it clattered, harmless now without its master to command it.

The castle gave a giant jolt and began to quake and crumble more violently than ever. Huge stones and timber fell all around Toby, catching aflame. He was trapped. The only way out was through the window, but he would never survive such a fall…

And then, through the smoke outside the window, a light shone. The light grew nearer and nearer until it penetrated the smoke and shadows and he could see what it was. Amanda Danielle walked on the air, her eyes fixed steadily upon his, her feet creating a path of light wherever she stepped. White light illuminated her, flowed from her, and reached to him.

Finally, she reached the window, stretching out both hands. He took her hands in his, and she led him out onto the path of light, their eyes never straying from each other. Toby searched her eyes, not daring to blink, as if he stood in a dream. Never did he feel so fearful to awaken from a dream. Though glistening with tears, her eyes flooded with love. The love that shone in them so many years ago still lingered. Yet that love radiated stronger now, as his love for her burned stronger even though they'd been apart for so long. At last, Amiel brought them together again.

As they stood on the bridge of light, reunited, Toby took Amanda Danielle in his arms and kissed her, fervently, deeply, all the love in the world flowing from the depths of his heart, into his lips and into her own.

Down below, the Armies of Darkness lay vanquished. As Rorrim's castle collapsed with a final quake, the Armies of Light, including Aaron who held Chasmira tight, looked up and saw Tobias, the rightful king, finally returned to his kingdom with his chosen queen, Amanda Danielle, standing beside each other, smiling. Together, they descended the path of light.

CHAPTER 26

The grand, double doors of the church sanctuary opened wide, allowing the couples to stream through. Pastyre White and Tobias already stood at the altar, Toby anxiously waiting and watching.

Mr. Root's little son and daughter, five-year-old Will and three-year-old Mattie, the ring bearer and flower girl, flounced in first. Both looked adorable, and Will wore a mischievous grin. Earlier that morning, he told his dad, "If I wear this tux today, none of the girls will be able to resist me." Mr. Root merely shook his head and mumbled, "I don't know where he gets this stuff at five-years-old…"

The bridesmaids and groomsmen followed, seven of each wearing a color corresponding to one of the seven colors of Prismatic's flag, except the best man, Caleb, and maid of honor, Ally, who wore pure white.

Next, Labrier and her husband followed in royal purple; Aaron and Chasmira in riveting indigo; Rachel and Nathan in stunning blue; Hailey and Sam in lively green; Josh and Krystal in cheery yellow—Josh had tried to tell Sam the wrong date of the wedding so he could lead two girls, both Krystal and Hailey, down the aisle; consequently, Krystal wasn't talking to him right now and walked down the aisle with a rather annoyed expression—Caleb and Tiffany in bright orange; and Taylor and Anyta in vivid red.

As the organ began to play the Butterfly Fantasia, grandly and magnificently, everyone arose as Amanda Danielle appeared beneath the arched doorway.

Her hair swirled up and glistened in an array of rosy-golden curls, a sparkling tiara nestled within them. Nothing glistened brighter than her eyes, brilliant, alternating shades of blue, violet, and green. Not in such a long while did they glitter with such sincere happiness.

Her dress stretched long, silky, glittering. The sheer white material overlaid a dress holding every color of the spectrum, the bright colors showing through where the white slit open in the middle. Her train and veil were embroidered with a shimmering, rainbow thread, and she carried in her small, slim hands a bouquet of spectrum-colored flowers.

Finally, she reached the altar and stood to face Toby, beaming at him like a thousand suns.

"And who gives this woman to be married?" Pastyre White asked, and then smirked. "Oh, I suppose that would be me."

"And I," reminded Mrs. White, casting him a look that warned he better not forget her, of all people.

The ceremony continued, Amanda Danielle gazing into Toby's eyes all the while. So many times her eyes filled with tears, but not tears of sorrow, only joy, relief, and thankfulness to Amiel for finally reuniting her with her beloved Toby.

As all the girls watched, they cried too, and tears even shone in Josh's eyes, though he would later inform everyone that he was "misting, not crying."

Finally, the exchanging of both vows and rings arrived, and Pastyre White declared, "What Amiel hath joined together, let no man put asunder. I now pronounce you husband and wife. You may indeed kiss the bride."

Amanda Danielle and Toby beamed at each other before kissing that long-awaited kiss. But as they kissed, a stream of light fell down upon them, white sparkles swirling about them like stardust, and suddenly, Toby's face healed, made whole. Aaron glanced over at Labrier who grinned at him. Aaron smiled to himself. He knew she healed Toby, knowing also by personal experience that she was an excellent healer.

Toby then swept Amanda Danielle off her feet, carrying her in his arms down the aisle. Everyone else followed outside, some with teary eyes but all with joyful hearts, to attend the reception set up in the garden.

* * *

Tiffany downed her third piece of wedding cake absent-mindedly. The need for sugar was two-fold, to spare herself from intense depression and madness as Caleb White spouted off endlessly of his latest antics, proudly holding out his chest as if he really expected that by doing so he could snag a girl less shallow than a rain puddle, and also because she searched for someone else, someone she truly desired to see, someone whose conversation was always less scarce yet always deeper, especially the words of his eyes. Someone she invited knowing the celebration would be at nightfall, when the shadows of night he was more akin to could better sheath his presence.

"Oh, yeah, did I mention those shrinking socks that Kelsey..."

Caleb's voice faded and she let slip a slight gasp, craning her neck, straining her eyes to see the distant white spot floating between the passing crowds. As the dancing couples swirled aside, there he stood. His black suit nearly merged with the shadows as though his luminous head floated alone like one of the diamond stars above, smiling, night-onyx eyes glittering, beckoning her. Her heart thrilled, tremoring like the strings of the harp playing. He seldom smiled, and now his smile was for her alone. He didn't blink, his eyes locked steadily on hers every time the crowds cleared. She started forward, slipping through the waltzing couples, Caleb's call but a fuzzy, indistinguishable blur.

At last, she stood before him, her eyes locked, spellbound upon his—

"Hey!" she shouted irritably as someone knocked roughly into her, breaking her gaze. It was Aaron and Chasmira racing into the confines of the trees. Aaron called over his shoulder, "Sorry Tiff! You too, Drizzle, glad to see you abandoning your hermitage, good luck finding a new hobby!"

Tiff glared at Aaron, hearing a small snicker escape Chasmira. Then she smirked, knowing Chasmira would scold him later, even if she couldn't help laughing at the moment. Despite his cockiness—or perhaps because of it—Chasmira could never help laughing at his wit, no matter how much it poked fun at a person.

Looking up at Dristann hopefully, she sighed relief as the smile still lingered upon his lips. He watched the couples gliding gracefully upon the moonlit grass. *None could quite possess his great fluidity*, she thought proudly though with a blush.

Glancing sideways at her, he shrugged. "Everyone else is doing it. May as well follow the crowd."

With a grin, she followed him into the woods.

After they walked far enough that the sounds of the party receded to muffled laughter and muddled melodies, he slowed their pace to a turtle's stroll. "You know, I heard how much you helped. Healing that wall and all that. Not to mention what you probably did invisibly. You're too nice, you know. Why do you choose to remain anonymous?"

She shrugged. "I don't for every story, but...with this one there's just so many people, so much going on. Sometimes, it's easier not to reveal anything that way. People ask you questions, even if accidentally, if they know you know the plot...

"Besides, it doesn't really matter. I help people because I like to, because Amiel would have me to..."

"Hmm...and Amiel would have you make yourself known to a rogue like me alone?"

"You were always my favorite, I told you that. And so you were always the one I wanted to make a real difference for. Usually, I throw myself into the thick of the story, enjoy every aspect I can. But I felt some connection, a *need*, a longing to focus on you, Dristann. The others...they don't need my help as much. But *you*...you *need* someone..."

"Don't know about that," he said nonchalantly. "But it *does* feel good having someone about all the same..."

His cool hand slipped into hers, radiating a pulsing warmth through the deepest crevices of her heart and soul. She prayed that he might see his need someday, before the day that approached too fast drew too near...

* * *

Chasmira stood under the tree that still held the phoenix nest—the phoenixes were grown and gone by now—watching as Amanda Danielle and Toby waltzed across the clearing. Aaron came up beside her and she said softly, "Well, you were right."

"Right?" he asked. "About what?"

"You said this would become a special place someday. Nothing could be more special than seeing the two of them together at last."

Aaron nodded. But his eyes did not linger on the dancing couple as Chasmira's did. His eyes shone on Chasmira alone. He moved a step closer to her, but suddenly, Rachel called her over.

She smiled. "I'll be right back." As Aaron watched her walk away, a feeling fluttered within him, an inkling that this place would grow yet more special to them as time went on.

EPILOGUE

Finally the day they had all been waiting for, both with excitement, yet with sorrow, arrived. It was time for Amanda Danielle and Toby to depart for Prismatic to start their new life together.

The whole school gathered on the eastern shore, where the lily-clad ship awaited to carry the new king and queen to their new kingdom. It was early morning. The sun was just preparing to rise, and the lilies of the ship had not yet opened.

Mr. Root made everyone bow their heads, and altogether they prayed for Amanda Danielle and Toby, asking Amiel to bless them with a safe journey.

Then came the part they all dreaded—the good-byes.

Amanda Danielle bid good-bye to each of the students and staff members in turn, hugging each as she cried, thanking them for all they'd done for her, reassuring them that all her love and prayers would go with them.

Finally, Amanda Danielle reached the last few, hugging them close in turn—Josh, Krystal, Tiff, Nathan, Rachel, Hailey, Sam, and lastly, Aaron and Chasmira. Yet how could they express to her all that their hearts felt at that moment? How could they thank her for all she'd done for them and tell her the things they would miss about her most—her laughter, her kindness, her sweetness, her sincere Amielian spirit, her encouragement and guidance?

But as Amanda Danielle saw the tears shining in their eyes, she understood. She put her arms around each of them, holding each tightly as she promised that her prayers and love would always remain with them.

Then, with a final wave, Amanda Danielle joined Toby, and together, they walked up the gangplank. Everyone watched with tears glistening down their cheeks.

Yet, as Amanda Danielle boarded the ship, she prepared to sail to a new life, a new world, on a new adventure. She would begin a family of her own, and she would be the greatest queen the Prismatic Isle had ever known or ever would know.

As the ship began to drift slowly from the shore, the sun rose over the horizon. As its light touched the lilies, their petals unfurled and blossomed, and from each shone tiny rays of prismatic light. As the sun rose higher, it lighted upon

Toby's head, and the prismatic colors of his hair merged to form pure, white light. Amanda Danielle's curls glistened with a rosy hue. The colors of their royal, rainbow robes also merged into whiteness. The last glimpse the students caught of Toby and Amanda Danielle was of them clad in white, pure light shining all about them and from them, the brightest lights shimmering from within their hearts.

Just before they slipped from beyond view, the king and queen lifted their hands in a final wave, and all on shore did the same.

When they completely faded from view, Mr. Root asked everyone to bow their heads, and they prayed once more for the couple's safe journey. Then everyone turned towards the woods and started back to school to begin the new day.

THE AMIELIAN LEGACY

Throughout the series, readers may notice references to random subjects they do not quite understand, such as "the Mass" or even "the Dark Enchantress." Well, don't worry, you're not going crazy! The reason for this is because *The Hero Chronicles* is actually a part of an over-arching, larger collection entitled *The Amielian Legacy*. So, to get the whole picture and see how everything intertwines, be sure to pick up the rest of the books as they are released!

~Christine E. Schulze

The Stregoni Sequence *(Four-book collection)*

The Chronicles of the Mira

The Hero Chronicles *(Five-book collection)*

The Gailean Quartet *(Four-book collection)*

Loz *(Three-book collection)*

The Legends of Surprisers Series *(Three-book collection)*

The Pirates of Meleeon

The Crystal Rings

Bloodmaiden

Lily in the Snow and Other Elemental Tales

Chimes, La Mariposa: Two Tales of Emreal

The Last Star

StarChild

Follow Me

Black Lace

The Boy Who Fell From the Sky

Tears of a Vampire Prince: the First Krystine *(A companion to The Stregoni Sequence)*

Carousel in the Clouds

THE HERO CHRONICLES